'Forgive me,' he ~~said,~~ **ragged with desire** ~~'I had no right~~ **to do that, no right at all.'**

'No,' Beatrice said quietly. 'Nor I to let you. We both know that your duty lies with Olivia, my lord. You are fond of her, and she would make you a fitting wife. Your position demands that, and I have never mixed in society. I am a plain, simple countrywoman, with none of the social arts...'

'As if that mattered...you cannot think it, Beatrice?'

'I do not know what to think,' she said. 'Please, my lord, let me go now. I must return to my sister. To stay longer might prove dangerous for both of us.'

A young woman disappears.
A husband is suspected of murder.
Stirring times for all the neighbourhood in

The STEEPWOOD
Scandal

Book 1

When the debauched Marquis of Sywell won
Steepwood Abbey years ago at cards, it led to the death
of the then Earl of Yardley. Now he's caused scandal
again by marrying a girl out of his class—and young
enough to be his granddaughter! After being married
only a short time, the Marchioness has disappeared,
leaving no trace of her whereabouts. There is every
expectation that yet more scandals will emerge, though
no one yet knows just how shocking they will be.

The four villages surrounding the Steepwood Abbey
estate are in turmoil, not only with the dire goings-on
at the Abbey, but also with their own affairs. Each
story in **The Steepwood Scandal** follows the mystery
behind the disappearance of the young woman, and the
individual romances of lovers connected in some way
with the intrigue.

Regency Drama
intrigue, mischief...and marriage

Lord
RAVENSDEN'S
MARRIAGE

Anne Herries

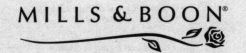
MILLS & BOON®

First published in Great Britain 2001
Harlequin Mills & Boon Limited,
Eton House, 18-24 Paradise Road, Richmond, Surrey TW9 1SR

© Harlequin Books S.A. 2001

Special thanks and acknowledgement are given to Anne Herries for her contribution to The Steepwood Scandal series

ISBN 0 263 82842 5

Set in Times Roman 10½ on 12½ pt.
119-0501-61523

Printed and bound in Spain
by Litografia Rosés S.A., Barcelona

Anne Herries lives in Cambridge but spends part of the winter in Spain, where she and her husband stay in a pretty resort nestled amid the hills that run from Malaga to Gibraltar. Gazing over a sparkling blue ocean, watching the sunbeams dance like silver confetti on the restless waves, Anne loves to dream up her stories of laughter, tears and romantic lovers.

Anne Herries' second novel in **The Steepwood Scandal**, *Counterfeit Earl,* follows Olivia's story. Coming soon.

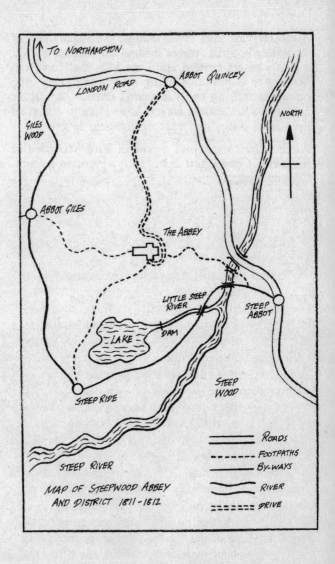

MAP OF STEEPWOOD ABBEY
AND DISTRICT 1811 - 1812

Chapter One

October, 1811

'Courage, Beatrice! Are you to be daunted by tales of dragons and witches? No, certainly not,' she answered herself, unconsciously speaking the words aloud. 'This is nonsense, sheer nonsense! Papa would be ashamed of you.'

Beatrice shivered, pulling her cloak more tightly about her body as the mischievous wind tried to tug it from her. She was approaching the gates of Steepwood Abbey from the eastern side, having just come from the village of Steep Abbot, which clustered outside the Abbey's crumbling walls at the point where the river entered its grounds.

In the village behind her lay the peaceful beauty of gracious trees, their bluish-green fronds brushing the edges of an idyllic pool in the river's course. Ahead of her in the gathering dusk was the great, squat, brooding shape of the ancient Abbey, its grounds almost a wasteland these days. It was not a pleasant place at the best of times, but at dusk it took on a menacing atmosphere that was as much a product of superstitious minds as of fact.

'There is not the least need to be nervous,' she told herself as she peered into the shadowy grounds. 'What was it Master Shakespeare said? Ah yes! *Our fears do make us traitors*. Do not be a traitor to your own convictions, Beatrice. It is all careless talk and superstition…'

But there were so many tales told about this place, and all of them calculated to make the blood run cold.

The land had been granted to the monks in the thirteenth century, and the Abbey had been built in a beautiful wooded area bordering the River Steep. Its origins were mystical, and it was held in popular belief that there had once, long centuries past, been a Roman temple somewhere in the grounds. Some of the stories told about the goings on at the Abbey were enough to make strong men turn pale.

So perhaps it was not just the chill of autumn air that made Beatrice shiver and turn cold as she paused to take her bearings.

'Foolish woman! This is autumn,' Beatrice scolded herself, 'and you ought to have remembered the nights were pulling in. You should have left half an hour sooner!'

It was now the fourth week of October, in the year of Our Lord 1811, and the nights had begun to pull in more quickly than she had imagined possible. She ought in all conscience to have set out on her journey home to the small village of Abbot Giles at least half an hour sooner.

Most sensible females who lived in one of the four villages that lay to the north, south, east and west of the Abbey would not have considered crossing the Abbey's land after dusk, or—since the Marquis of Sywell had taken up residence some eighteen years earlier—during the day for that matter!

Beatrice Roade, however, was made of sterner stuff. At the age of twenty-three she was of course a confirmed spinster, the first flush of her youth behind her (though not forgotten!), all hope of ever marrying denied her. She was tall, well-formed, with an easy way of walking that proclaimed her the healthy, no-nonsense woman she was. Attractive, her features strong, classical, with rather haunting green eyes and hair the colour of burnished chestnuts, she was thought slightly daunting by the local squires, who did not care for her cleverness—or her humour, which was oft-times baffling.

'Miss Roade,' they were wont to say of her as she was seen walking between the four villages, 'bookish, you know. And as for looks—not the patch of her sister Miss Olivia. Now she is a beauty!'

And this from men who could hardly have caught more than a fleeting glimpse of Miss Olivia for the past fifteen years! But Miss Olivia took after her mother, and *she* had been beautiful. Miss Roade was like her father's family no doubt, and known to be sensible.

So what was the very sensible Beatrice doing poised at the gate to Steepwood's boundary walls, a gate which lay drunkenly open and rusting, useless these many years? Could she really be contemplating taking a short cut?

If they entered the grounds at all, most local folk stayed well away from the Abbey itself, taking either the path which led past the Little Steep river and the lake, or skirting Giles Wood—though only the braver amongst the villagers went near the woods.

There were odd goings on in the woods! Nan had told her that people were talking about it. Lights had been seen there at night again recently, and the gossips were saying that the Marquis was up to his old tricks—for it was firmly believed that when he had first come to the Abbey, Sywell and his friends had cavorted naked with their whores amongst the trees—and they had worn animal masks on their heads!

'Scandalous! That a nobleman of England should behave in such a manner,' Nan had said only that morning as she polished the sofa table in the parlour until the beautiful wood gleamed so that she could see her reflection. 'I dread to think what may be going on there.'

'Nan, you intrigue me,' Beatrice had teased. 'Just what dire things do you imagine are happening up there?'

'Nothing that you or I should want to know about,' her aunt had told her with a look of mock severity.

Really, the Marquis's behaviour was too disgusting to mention—except that life was sometimes a little slow in the villages, and it did make such a delightful tale to whisper of to one's friends.

Ghislaine and Beatrice had laughed together that

very afternoon, though Ghislaine had been inclined to dismiss the rumours.

'The Marquis of Sywell is too old for such games,' she said, her eyes dancing with mischief. 'Surely it cannot be true, Beatrice?'

'I would not have thought so—though there must be something going on. The lights have been seen by several villagers.'

'Well, I imagine there will be some simple explanation,' Ghislaine had said, and Beatrice nodded. 'I dare say the lights are but lanthorns carried by some person with business on the estate.'

'Yes, I am sure you must be right—but the gossips invent so many stories. It is amusing, is it not?'

Amusing then, but not quite so funny when Beatrice was faced with a walk through the wasteland that was now the Abbey grounds.

Some might whisper of devil-worship and the black arts, but others spoke of pagan rites that were firmly rooted in the history of ancient Britons. It was said that in the old days virgins had been sacrificed on a stone by the lake, and their blood used to bring fertility to the land. Naturally Beatrice was too intelligent to let such tales weigh with her. Really, what did go on in the minds of some people!

Besides, the Abbey had long been the home of an old and respected family—it was only since it had fallen into the hands of the Marquis of Sywell that it had become a place of abomination to the people of the four villages.

Beatrice took heart from the sensible view of her friend. Strange goings on there might be, but they were unlikely to be anything that could bring harm to her.

'It is foolish to be frightened just because it is becoming dark,' Beatrice murmured to herself. 'If I but walk quickly I shall be home in less than half an hour.'

Beatrice glanced up at the sky. Storm clouds were gathering. If she took the longer route, she might be caught and drenched by the rain that was certainly coming. She was not to be frightened by rumour and superstition. She would take the shorter route that crossed the Marquis's grounds close to the Abbey itself. It was a risk, of course, because she would have to pass close to that part of the building which was now used as a private home.

'Nothing ventured, nothing gained.' Beatrice murmured one of her beloved father's maxims, conveniently forgetting that he had so often been proved wrong in the past. For it was Mr Bertram Roade's tendency to plunge into the unknown that had led to his losing the small but adequate competence which had been settled on him by his maternal grandfather— Lord Borrowdale. 'What can *he* do to me after all?'

The *he* she was thinking of was, of course, the wicked Marquis himself, of whom the tales were so many and so lurid that Beatrice found them amusing rather than frightening—at least at home and in daylight.

'Be sensible,' Beatrice told herself fiercely as she began to cross the gravel drive which would take her past the Abbey—and the dark, haunting ruins of the Chapter House, which had been destroyed at the time of the dissolution of the monasteries and never restored. 'He couldn't possibly have done everything they say; otherwise he would have died of the pox or some similar foul disease long ago.' She smiled at the inelegance of her own words. 'Oh, Beatrice! What would dear Mrs Guarding say if she knew what you were thinking now?'

It was because she had spent the afternoon at Mrs Guarding's excellent school for young ladies that she was having to risk venturing right to the heart of the Abbey grounds now.

It had been so pleasant for the time of year earlier that afternoon. Beatrice had visited her friend Mademoiselle Ghislaine de Champlain, who was the French mistress at Mrs Guarding's school, and had stopped to drink tea with her.

Beatrice had been fortunate enough to spend one precious year as a teacher/pupil at the school, where she had studied with Ghislaine to improve her knowledge and pronunciation of French, in return for helping the younger pupils with their English—the happiest year of her life.

It was, of course, the only way she could afford to attend the exclusive school, her education having been undertaken by her father at home, which might account for some of the very odd things she had been taught.

She had been twenty during that precious year spent at the exclusive establishment. Beatrice had hoped to make a niche for herself at the school, because she very much admired the principles of the moral but advanced-thinking woman who ran it.

However, family duties had forced her to return to her home.

Thinking about the illness and subsequent death of her dearest mother occupied Beatrice's thoughts as she walked, banishing all lingering echoes of orgies and dire goings on at the Abbey. Mrs Roade had been an acknowledged beauty in her day, and, as the only sister of the wealthy Lord Burton, had been expected to marry well. Her decision to accept Bertram Roade had been a disappointment to her family.

Beatrice's musings were brought to an abrupt end as she heard the scream. It was the most blood-curdling, terrifying sound she had ever heard in her life, and she whirled round, looking for its source.

It had seemed to come from the Abbey itself. Perhaps the chapel or the cloisters...but she could not be certain. It might have come from somewhere in the grounds. Yes, surely it must have been the grounds—an animal caught in a trap perhaps? So thought the sensible Miss Roade.

For an instant, Beatrice considered the possibility of a dreadful crime...possibly murder or rape. Vague memories flitted through her mind; there was a tale of a girl caught inside the grounds one night when the monks still lived there: it was said that the girl had been found dead in the morning!

Beatrice shivered and increased her pace, her nerves tingling. All the stories of the Marquis's atrocities came rushing back to fill her mind with vague fears of herself being attacked by...what?

Long dead monks? Ridiculous! What then? Hardly the Marquis? Surely she was not truly afraid of him?

He was after all married at last, to a rather beautiful, young—and if the little anyone knew of her was anything to go by, mysterious girl. All Beatrice knew of her was that her name was Louise, and that she had been adopted as a baby by the Marquis's bailiff, John Hanslope. It was whispered that she was his bastard, but no one knew the truth of the affair.

The scandal of the nobleman's marriage to his own bailiff's ward had both shocked and delighted the people of the four villages. Despite his terrible reputation, it was still unthinkable that a man of his background should marry a girl who was after all little more than a servant. 'Quite beyond the pale, my dear!'

Beatrice's own sympathies lay with the unfortunate girl who had married him, for surely she must have been desperate to do such a thing?

A sudden thought struck Beatrice—could it have been the Marquis's wife who had screamed? She glanced at the brooding, menacing shape of the Abbey and crossed herself superstitiously. What could *he* have been doing to her to make her scream like that?

'No, no,' she whispered. 'It could not have been her—nor any woman. It was an animal, only an animal.'

He *was* said to be in love…after years of wickedness and debauchery!

Even a man of the Marquis's calibre could not be capable of hurting the woman he loved—or could he?

Beatrice tucked her head down against the wind and began to run. Perhaps it was her anxiety to leave the grounds of the Abbey that made her careless? It was certain that she did not see or hear the pounding hooves of the great horse until it came rushing at her out of the darkness. She was directly in its path and had to throw herself aside to avoid being knocked over.

Her action led to her stumbling and, having the breath knocked from her body by the force of her fall, she could only continue to lie where she was as the rider galloped by, seemingly unaware or uncaring of the fact that he had almost ridden her down.

Beatrice caught only a glimpse of him as he passed, but she knew it was the wicked Marquis himself, riding as if the devil were after him. He was a big man, wrapped about by a black cloak, his iron-grey hair straggling and unkempt about his shoulders. An ugly creature by all accounts, his features thickened and coarsened by his excesses—though she herself had never caught more than a fleeting glimpse of him. He was a bruising rider, and she had sometimes seen him in the distance on her walks—but they were not acquainted. The Roade family did not move in his circles, nor he in theirs.

'That was not well done of you, sir,' Beatrice murmured as he and his horse disappeared into the darkness.

She rose to her feet a little unsteadily, her usual composure seriously disturbed by what had happened that night. It was certain that the Marquis was in a black mood, perhaps drunk, as the gossips said he often was. Beatrice shuddered as she thought of the young woman who had married him the previous

year. How terrible to be trapped in marriage with such
a monster!

What could have possessed her to do such a thing?

Beatrice had never met the young Marchioness, or
even seen her out walking. As far as Beatrice knew,
no one had seen much of her since the wedding.
People said she hardly left the Abbey—some said she
was too ashamed, some murmured of her being kept
a prisoner by her wicked husband, others that she was
ill…and there was little to wonder at in that, married
to such a brute!

She could only have married him for his money.
Everyone said it, and Beatrice was sure it must be the
truth—but had the Marquis been the richest man in
England, *she* would not have married such a monster!

Beatrice had stopped shaking. She resumed her
walk at a more sensible pace, keeping her head up so
that she was aware of what was in front of her. There
was little to be heard but the howl of the wind, which
was eerie and unpleasant.

She would be glad to be home!

'You're soaked to the skin, my love,' Nan said,
fussing over her the moment she entered her father's
house. 'We have been on the look for you this past
hour or more. Whatever do you mean by worrying
your poor father so?'

They progressed to the parlour, Beatrice having left
her sodden cloak in the hall. She moved closer to the
fire, holding her hands to the flames until she had
stopped shivering, then went over to the large oak and

upholstered Knole settee, carefully moving her aunt's embroidery before sitting down.

'Have I worried Papa?' Beatrice thought it improbable. Her father would most likely be in his study, working on one of his inventions—the marvellous, wholly useless objects he was forever wasting his time on, which he believed were going to restore his fortune one day. 'I think *you* were worried, Nan. Poor, dear Papa can hardly have noticed. Now, if I were not here for dinner—then he might begin to worry. Especially if it meant waiting for his meal.'

'Beatrice!' Nan scolded. 'Now that is unkind in you. I know your humour, my dear—but it sounds harsh in a young woman to be so cynical. It is little wonder that…' She broke off, biting her lip as she saw the look in her darling's eyes.

'Yes, I know I have driven them all away—all my suitors,' Beatrice said ruefully. 'I really should have taken Squire Rush, shouldn't I? He has three thousand a year, I dare say…but he has buried three wives and that brood of his was really too much!'

'There were others,' her aunt said. Mrs Nancy Willow was a widow in her early forties: a plump, comfortable, loving woman, who was extremely fond of her eldest niece. She had come to her brother's house only after her husband (a soldier turned adventurer) had died of a fever. She sometimes thought it would have been better if she had been there before her lovely but slightly bird-brained sister-in-law had died, but she and Eddie had been in India at the time. 'I understand there was a suitable admirer once…'

'And who told you that, aunt?'

Nan frowned. Beatrice rarely called her 'aunt' in just that way: she was clearly touching on a sore place.

'Well, well, it doesn't matter,' she said. 'But should another suitable young man come along…'

'I could not leave Papa,' Beatrice said at once. 'Besides, it will not happen. I am nearly at my last prayers.'

'Now that you are not!' Nan said. 'You have many qualities, Beatrice. A discerning man would know that the minute he laid eyes on you…'

'…and fall instantly in love with me?' Beatrice said, amused by her aunt's romantic notions. 'Only find me this suitor, Nan dearest—and, if he is not too dim-witted, which I think he may have to be, I will engage to do my best to snare him.'

'You and your wicked, wicked tongue,' her aunt said, smiling even as she shook her head. 'And as for not being able to leave your papa—you know that is not so. You were obliged to give up all thoughts of marriage when your mama fell ill. To have left your father then would have been careless in you—but my brother has been kind enough to offer me a home for the rest of my life…'

'Unless *you* receive an offer of marriage, Nan!'

Her aunt pulled a wry face. 'I could not be tempted. I am comfortable here, and here I shall stay. Since it does not take two of us to run this house, you are free to do as you wish…'

'Yes, I see that it makes a difference…' Beatrice looked serious. 'It might be better if I started to look for a position…Papa's funds are limited, and since…'

'He would never hear of it, and nor should I,' declared Nan roundly. 'If anyone should look elsewhere, it must be me.'

'No!' Beatrice spoke quickly. She had been afraid her aunt would take that attitude, which was why she had not spoken her thoughts aloud before this. 'You do not understand, Nan. I am not speaking of hiring myself out as a governess or a companion…I would only leave here if I could go back to Mrs Guarding's school as a teacher.'

Her aunt stared at her, eyes narrowing. 'Is that why you have been so long this afternoon?'

'No, indeed, for I have not yet spoken to Mrs Guarding about my idea. I went to see Ghislaine de Champlain, who, as I told you, is the French mistress there. We spent some time talking, and then had tea together in her room, which overlooks the river. It really was most pleasant.'

'You speak of Mademoiselle Champlain often—and of the time you spent at the school,' Nan said. 'Would it really make you happy to return there, dearest?'

'Yes, I think so,' Beatrice replied, smothering a sigh. It wasn't that she was unhappy with her life in her father's house, but she sometimes longed for some stimulating company—a friend she could sharpen her wits on now and then without feeling that she was either hurting or bewildering that friend.

She briefly remembered her long-dashed hopes, which had been destroyed when she was a girl of nineteen—just the same age as her sister was now!—but their situations had been very different. Olivia was

in London enjoying a brilliant season, and engaged to
one of the best 'catches' of the Season. For Beatrice
there had been no Season, and only one suitor she
might have taken—if he had asked. However, after
toying with her hopes and affections for a whole
month one summer, he had taken himself back off to
London and proposed to an heiress!

'Pray do not look so sad, my love,' Nan said.
'Come, sit by the fire and let me dry your poor feet.
You look as if you have had a tumble in the mud!'

'As a matter of fact, I have,' Beatrice said, forgetting her disappointments as she recalled what had
happened to her that evening. 'I walked home through
the Abbey grounds, Nan.'

'You never did!' Nan looked horrified. 'Never say
that monster attacked you?'

'In a way,' Beatrice replied, then shook her head
as Nan looked fit to faint. 'Oh, nothing like that. I
heard something…a scream, I think…then this horse
and rider came up out of the darkness and I was
forced to throw myself out of his path. Had I not done
so, I must have been crushed beneath the hooves of
the horse. I am sure it was the Marquis himself, and
in a fearful mood.'

Nan crossed herself instinctively. Neither she nor
any member of her family were Catholics, but in a
matter such as this, the action could be very comforting.

Beatrice laughed as she saw her aunt's reaction. 'I
must admit to doing much the same as you when I
heard the scream,' she admitted. 'It was the most hor-
rifying sound imaginable…' She broke off as their

one little maid came into the room, carrying a silver salver. 'Yes, Lily—what is it?'

'Bellows fetched this letter for you from the receiving office this afternoon, Miss Roade. It's from London.'

'Then it must be from Olivia,' Beatrice said, feeling a flicker of excitement. 'Perhaps it is an invitation to the wedding at last.'

The longcase clock in the hall was striking the hour of five as Beatrice took the sealed packet from her servant.

Beatrice had been anxiously awaiting the invitation since learning from her sister that she was about to become engaged to Lord Ravensden, the wealthy Lord Burton's heir. Not that Lord Burton's wealth was of any interest to his heir, who, according to rumour, already had far more money than any one person could possibly need.

Olivia had been adopted by their rich relatives when she was a child. She had been loved and petted by them ever since, living a very different life from her elder sister, who had been overlooked by Lord and Lady Burton when they agreed to take one of the children as their own.

The sisters' parting had devastated Beatrice, who, being the elder, had understood what was happening, and why. She had kept in touch by letter since the day Olivia was taken away, but they had met only twice since then, when her mother's sister-in-law had brought Olivia on brief visits. Having seen the engagement announced in *The Times*, which her papa continued to subscribe to despite his meagre funds,

Beatrice had expected to hear from her sister almost daily, and was beginning to think she was to be left out of the celebrations.

She ripped the small packet open eagerly, then read its contents three times before she could believe what she was seeing. It was not possible! Olivia must be funning her...surely she must? If this was not a jest...it did not bear thinking of!

'Is something the matter?' asked Nan. 'You look upset, Beatrice. Has something happened to your sister?'

'It is most distressing,' Beatrice said, sounding as shocked as she felt. 'I cannot believe this, Nan. Olivia writes to tell me that she will not now be marrying Lord Ravensden. She has decided she cannot like him sufficiently...and has told him of her decision.'

'You mean she has jilted him?' Nan stared at her in dismay. 'How could she? She will be ruined. Has she no idea of the consequences of her actions?'

'I think she must have.' Beatrice gave a little cry of distress as she read over the page something she had missed earlier. 'Oh, no! This is the most terrible news. Lord and Lady Burton have...disowned her. They say she has disgraced them, and they will no longer harbour a viper in their home...'

'That is a little harsh, is it not?' Nan wrinkled her brow. 'What she has done is wrong, no one could deny that—but I should imagine Olivia must have her reasons. She would not do such a thing out of caprice—would she?'

'No, of course not,' Beatrice defended her sister

loyally. 'We do not know each other well—but I am sure she is not so cruel.'

'What can have prevailed upon her to accept him if she did not mean to go through with the marriage?' Nan asked, shaking her head in wonder. Jilting one's fiancé was not something to be undertaken lightly— and a man as rich as Lord Ravensden into the bargain!

'She says she has realised that she cannot be happy as his wife,' Beatrice said, frowning over her sister's hurried scrawl. 'And that she was cruelly deceived in his feelings for her.'

'What will she do now?'

'Lord Burton has told her she has one week to leave his house—so she asks if she may come here.'

'Come here?' Nan stared at her in dismay. 'Does she realise how we go on here? She will find it very different to what she has been used to, Beatrice.'

'Yes, I fear she will,' Beatrice replied. 'However, I shall speak to Papa at once, and then, if he agrees, I shall write and tell her she is welcome in this house.'

'My brother will agree to whatever you suggest,' Nan said a little wryly. 'You must know that?'

Beatrice smiled, knowing that she always without fail managed to twist her father round her finger. He could refuse her nothing, for the simple reason that he was able to give her very little. Fortunately, Beatrice had a tiny allowance of her own, which came to her directly from a bequest left to her by her maternal grandmother, Lady Anne Smith.

Nan had given her a towel to dry herself, and Beatrice had used it to good effect. Her long hair was wild about her face, gleaming with reddish gold lights and giving her a natural beauty she had never noticed for herself. She handed the towel back to her aunt, and looked down at herself. Her gown was disgraceful, but her dear, forgetful papa would probably never notice.

'You realise Olivia will be an added burden on your father's slender income?' Nan warned. 'You have little enough for yourself as it is.'

'My sister will be destitute if we do not take her in,' Beatrice replied, frowning. 'I do not know whether they have cast her off without a penny—but it sounds as if they may have done so. It would be cruel indeed of me if I were to refuse to let her shelter in her own home.'

'Yes, and something *you* could never do,' Nan said warmly. 'I have no objections, my love. I only wish you to think before you leap—unlike my poor brother.'

'We shall manage,' Beatrice said, and left her aunt with a smile.

The smile was wiped out the instant she left the room. She had not mentioned anything to Nan, because it was still not clear to her exactly what her sister's rather terse words had meant—but clearly Lord Ravensden was not a man Olivia could love or respect. Indeed, if Beatrice was not mistaken, he was a hard, ruthless man who cared for little else but wealth and duty.

He had had the cold-hearted effrontery to tell one of his friends that he was marrying to oblige Lord Burton. Since the Burtons had no children of their own, the title and fortune would pass by entail to a distant cousin of Lord Burton. They had felt this was a little unfair on the daughter they had adopted, and so made their wishes known to Lord Burton's heir: it would please them if he were to marry the girl they had lavished with affection since she came to them.

Apparently, Lord Ravensden had proposed to Olivia, giving her the impression that he cared for her—and it was only by accident that she had learned the truth. It must have distressed her deeply!

No wonder she had declared herself unable to love him. If Beatrice were not much mistaken, it would push any woman to the limits to find a place in her heart for such an uncaring man.

She wished that she might have him at her mercy for five minutes! It would give her the greatest pleasure to tell him exactly what she thought of him.

Chapter Two

Beatrice fought her rising temper. She was slow to anger, but when something offended her strong sense of justice—as it did now—she could be awesome in her fury.

'If I could but get my hands on him!' she muttered furiously. 'He should see how it feels to be treated so harshly. I should make him suffer as he makes my poor sister.'

No, no, this would not do! She must appear calm and cheerful when speaking to Papa. He had so many worries, the poor darling. This burden must not be allowed to fall on his shoulders. As for the added strain on his slender income...well, it made the idea of her becoming a teacher at Mrs Guarding's school even more necessary. If she could support herself, her father would be able to spare a few guineas a year for Olivia to dress herself decently—though not, her sister feared, in the manner to which she had become accustomed.

Beatrice paused outside the door to her father's

study, then knocked and walked in without waiting for an answer. It would have done her little good to wait. Mr Roade was engrossed in the sets of charts and figures on his desk, and would not have heard her.

Like many men of the time, he was fascinated with the sciences and the invention of all kinds of ingenious devices. Mr Roade was a great admirer of James Watt, who had invented the miraculous steam engine, which had begun to be used in so many different ways. And, of course, Mr Robert Fulton, the American, who had first shown his splendid steam boat on the Seine in France in 1803. Bertram Roade was certain that his own designs would one day make him a great deal of money.

'Papa…' Beatrice said, walking up to glance over his shoulder. He was working on an ingenious design for a fireplace that would heat a water tank fitted behind it and provide a constant supply of hot water for the household. It was a splendid idea, if only it would work. Unfortunately, the last time her father had persuaded someone to manufacture the device for him, it had overheated and blown apart, causing a great deal of damage and costing more than a hundred pounds, both to repair the hole in the kitchen wall and to repay the money invested by an outraged partner. Money they could ill afford.

'May I speak with you a moment?'

'I've nearly got the puzzle solved,' Mr Roade replied, not having heard her. 'I'm sure I know why it exploded last time…you see the air became too hot and there was nowhere for it to escape. Now, if I had a valve which let out the steam before it built up…'

'Yes, Papa, I'm sure you are right.'

Mr Roade looked up. Beatrice was usually ready to argue his theories with him; he was none too sure that his most recent was correct, and had hoped to discuss it with her.

'You wanted to talk to me, my dear?' His mild eyes blinked at her from behind the gold-rimmed spectacles that were forever in danger of falling off his nose. 'It isn't time for dinner—is it?'

'No, Papa, not quite. I came to see you about another matter.' She took a deep breath. 'Olivia wishes to come and stay with us. I would like your permission to write and tell her she will be welcome here for as long as she wishes.'

'Olivia…your sister?' He wrinkled his brow, as if searching for something he knew he must have forgotten. A smile broke through as he remembered. 'Ah yes, she is to be married. No doubt she wishes for a chance to have a little talk with her sister before her wedding.'

'No, Papa. It isn't quite like that. For reasons Olivia will make clear to us, she has decided not to marry Lord Ravensden. She wants to come and live here.'

'Are you sure you have that right, m'dear?' Mr Roade looked bewildered. 'I thought it was a splendid match—the man's as rich as Midas, ain't he?'

'That is a very apt description, Father. For if you remember, Midas was the King of Phrygia whose touch turned all to gold, and on whom Apollo bestowed the ears of an ass. Lord Ravensden must be a fool to have turned Olivia against him, but it seems, like that ancient king, he cares more for gold than the sweetness of a woman's touch.'

'Must be a fool then,' sighed a man who had loved his wife too much. 'Olivia is better off without him. Write at once and tell her we shall be delighted to have her home. Never did think it was a good idea for her to go away…your mother's idea. She wanted the chance of a better life for at least one of her daughters, and her poor sister-in-law was childless. Thank God the Burtons didn't pick you! I couldn't have borne that loss, Beatrice.'

'Thank you, Papa.' She smiled and kissed his forehead lovingly. 'You know, if you let all the steam go in one direction, it might pass through pipes before it finally escapes, and give some heat to the rooms. It would make the bedrooms so much warmer…as long as you could be sure the device that heats the water will not blow up like it did the last time.'

'Let the steam pass through pipes that run round the house.' Mr Roade looked at his daughter as if she had just lit a candle in his head. 'That's a very good notion, Beatrice. It might look a little ugly, I suppose. I wonder if anyone would put up with that for the convenience of feeling warm?'

'I certainly would,' Beatrice replied. 'Have you made any advances on the grate for a smokeless fire? Mine was smoking dreadfully again last night. It always does when the wind is from the east.'

'It might be a bird's nest,' her father said. 'I'll sweep the chimney out for you tomorrow.'

'Thank you, Papa, but I'm sure Mr Rowley will come up from the village if we ask him. It is not fitting for you to undertake such tasks.' *Besides which, her father would make a dreadful mess of it!*

'Fiddlesticks!' Mr Roade said. 'I'll do it for you first thing tomorrow.'

'Very well, Papa.'

Beatrice smiled as she went away. Her father would have forgotten about the smoking chimney five minutes after she left him, which mattered not at all, since she intended to send for the sweep when their one and only manservant next went down to Abbot Quincey to fetch their weekly supplies.

Seeing her father's manservant tending the candelabra on the lowboy in the hall, Beatrice smiled.

'Good evening, Bellows. It is a terrible evening, is it not?'

'We're in for a wild night, miss. Lily brought your letter?'

'Yes, thank you—and thank you for thinking to fetch it for me.'

'You're welcome, miss. I was in the market at Abbot Quincey and it was the work of a moment to see if any mail had come.'

She nodded and smiled, then passed on up the stairs.

It was possible to buy most goods from the general store in Abbot Quincey, which was much the largest of the four villages, and might even have been called a small town these days, but when anything more important was needed, they had to send Bellows to Northampton.

They were lucky to have Bellows, who was responsible for much of the work both inside the house and out. He had been with them since her father was a boy, and could remember when the Roade family had not been as poor as they were now.

For some reason all his own, Bellows was devoted to his master, and remained loyal despite the fact that he had not been paid for three years. He received his keep, and had his own methods of supplementing his personal income. Sometimes a plump rabbit or a pigeon found its way into the kitchen, and Beatrice suspected that Bellows was not above a little poaching, but she would never dream of asking where the gift came from. Indeed, she could not afford to!

Walking upstairs to her bedchamber to wash and change her clothes, Beatrice reflected on the strangeness of fate.

'My poor, dear sister,' she murmured. 'Oh, how could that rogue Ravensden have been so cruel?'

She herself had been deserted by a man who had previously declared himself madly in love with her, because, she understood, he had lost a small fortune at the gaming tables. She truly believed that Matthew Walters had intended to marry her, until he was ruined by a run of bad luck—he had certainly declared himself in love with her several times. Only her own caution had prevented her allowing her own feelings to show.

If she had given way to impulse, she would have been jilted publicly, which would have made her situation very much worse. At least *she* had been spared the scandal and humiliation that would have accompanied such an event.

Only Beatrice's parents had known the truth. Mrs Roade had held her while she wept out her disappointment and hurt…but that was a long time ago. Beatrice had been much younger then, perhaps a little naïve, innocent of the ways of the world. She had grown up very quickly after Matthew's desertion.

Since then, she had given little thought to marriage. She suspected that most men were probably like the one who had tried so ardently to seduce her. If she had been foolish enough to give in to his pleading…what then? She might have been ruined as well as jilted. Somehow she had resisted, though she had believed herself in love…

Beatrice laughed harshly. She was not such a fool as to believe in it now! She had learned to see the world for what it was, and knew that love was just something to be written of by dreamers and poets.

She had been taught a hard lesson, and now she had her sister's experience to remind her. If Olivia had been so hurt that she was driven to do something that she must know would ruin her in the eyes of the world… What a despicable man Lord Ravensden must be!

'Oh, you wicked, wicked man,' she muttered as she finished dressing and prepared to go down for dinner.

'I declare you deserve to be boiled in oil for what you have done!'

Lord Ravensden had begun to equate with the Marquis of Sywell in her mind. After her uncomfortable escape from injury that evening, Beatrice was inclined to think all the tales of *him* were true! And Lord Ravensden not much better.

A moment's reflection must have told her this was hardly likely to be true, for her sister would surely not even have entertained the idea of marriage to such a man. She was the indulged adopted daughter of loving parents, and had she said from the start that she could not like their heir, would surely have been excused from marrying him. It was the shock and the scandal of her having jilted her fiancé that had upset them.

However, Beatrice was not thinking like herself that evening. The double shock had made her somehow uneasy. She had the oddest notion that something terrible had either happened or was about to... something that might affect not only her and her sister's lives, but that of many others in the four villages.

The scream she had heard that night before the Marquis came rushing upon her...it had sounded evil. Barely human. Was it an omen of something?

After hearing it, she had come home to receive her sister's letter. Of course the scream could have nothing to do with that...and yet the feeling that the lives of many people were about to change was strong in her. A cold chill trickled down her spine as she wondered at herself. Never before had she experienced such a feeling…was it what people sometimes called a premonition?

Do not be foolish, Beatrice, she scolded herself mentally. Whatever would Papa say to such an illogical supposition?

Her dear papa would, she felt sure, give her a lecture upon the improbability of there being anything behind her feelings other than mere superstition, and of course he would be perfectly right.

Shaking her head, her hair now neatly confined in a sleek chignon, she dismissed her fears. There had been something about the atmosphere at the Abbey that night, but perhaps all old buildings with a history of mystery and violence would give out similar vibes if one visited them alone and at dusk.

If Beatrice had been superstitious, she would have said that her experience that evening was a warning— a sign from the ghosts of long dead monks—but she was not fanciful. She knew that what she had heard was most likely the cry of a wounded animal. Like the practical girl she was, she dismissed the idea of warnings and premonitions as nonsense, laughed at her own fancies and went downstairs to eat a hearty meal.

'Ravensden, you are an almighty fool, and should be ashamed of yourself! Heaven only knows how you are to extricate yourself from this mess.'

Gabriel Frederick Harold Ravensden, known as Harry to a very few, Ravensden to most, contemplated his image in his dressing-mirror and found himself disliking what he saw more than ever before. It was the morning of the thirty-first of October, and he was standing in the bedchamber of his house in Portland Place. What a damned ass he had been! He ought to be boiled in oil, then flayed until his bones showed through.

He grinned at the thought, wondering if it should really be the other way round to inflict the maximum punishment, then the smile was wiped clean as he remembered it was his damnable love of the ridiculous that had got them all into this mess in the first place.

'Did you say something, milord?' Beckett asked, coming into the room with a pile of starched neck-cloths in anticipation of his lordship's likely need. 'Will you be wearing the new blue coat this morning?'

'What? Oh, I'm not sure,' Harry said. 'No, I think something simpler—more suitable for riding.'

His man nodded, giving no sign that he thought the request surprising since his master had returned to town only the previous evening. He offered a fine green cloth, which was accepted by his master with an abstracted air. An unusual disinterest in a man famed for his taste and elegance in all matters of both dress and manners.

'You may leave me,' Harry said, after he had been helped into his coat, having tied a simple knot in the first neckcloth from the pile. 'I shall call you if I need you.'

'Yes, milord.'

Beckett inclined his head and retired to the dressing-room to sigh over the state of his lordship's boots after his return from the country, and Harry returned to the thorny problem on his mind.

He should in all conscience have told his distant cousin to go to hell the minute the marriage was suggested to him. Yet the beautiful Miss Olivia Roade Burton had amused him with her pouts and frowns. She had been *the* unrivalled success of the Season, and, having been thoroughly spoiled all her life, was inclined to be a little wayward.

However, her manners were so charming, her face so lovely, that he had been determined to win her favours. He had found the chase diverting, and thought he might like to have her for his wife—and a wife he must certainly have before too many months had passed.

'A damned, heavy-footed, crass idiot!' Harry muttered, remembering the letter he had so recently received from his fiancée. 'This business is of your own making...'

At four-and-thirty, he imagined he was still capable of giving his wife the son he so badly needed, but it would not do to leave it much later—unless he wanted the abominable Peregrine to inherit his own estate and that of Lord Burton. Both he and Lord Burton were agreed that such an outcome would not be acceptable to either of them—though at the moment they were agreeing on little else. Indeed, they had parted in acrimony. Had Harry not been a gentleman, he would probably have knocked the man down. He frowned as he recalled their conversation of the previous evening.

'An infamous thing, sir,' Harry had accused. 'To abandon a girl you have lavished with affection. I do not understand how you could turn her out. Surely you will reconsider?'

'She has been utterly spoilt,' Lord Burton replied. 'I have sent her to her family in Northamptonshire. Let her see how she likes living in obscurity.'

'Northamptonshire of all places! Good grief, man, it is the back of beyond, and must be purgatory for a young lady of fashion, who has been used to mixing in the best circles. Olivia will be bored out of her mind within a week!'

'I shall not reconsider until she remembers her duty to me,' Lord Burton had declared. 'I have cut off her allowance and shall disinherit her altogether if she does not admit her fault and apologise to us both.'

'I think that it is rather we who should apologise to her.'

After that, their conversation had regrettably gone downhill.

Harry was furious. Burton's conduct was despicable—and he, Harry Ravensden, had played a major part in the downfall of a very lovely young woman!

A careless remark in a gentleman's club, overheard by some malicious tongue—and he imagined he could guess the owner of that tongue! If he were not much mistaken, it was his cousin Peregrine Quindon who had started the vicious tale circulating. It was a

wicked piece of mischief, and Peregrine would hear
from him at some point in the future!

Olivia had clearly been hurt by some other young
lady's glee in the fact that her marriage was, after all,
merely one of convenience, that despite her glittering
Season, and being the toast of London society, her
bridegroom was marrying her only to oblige her
adopted father. She had reacted in a very natural way,
and had written him a stilted letter, telling him that
she had decided she could not marry him, which he
had received only on his return to town—by which
time the scandal had broken and was being whispered
of all over London.

Harry cursed the misfortune that had taken him
from town. He had been summoned urgently to his
estates in the north, a journey there and back of several days. Had he been in London, he might have seen
Olivia, explained that he did indeed have a very high
regard for her, and was honoured that she had accepted him—as he truly was.

Perhaps he had not fallen in love in the true romantic sense—but Harry did not really believe in that
kind of love. He had experienced passion often
enough, and also a deep affection for his friends, but
never total, heart-stopping love.

He enjoyed the company of intelligent women. His
best friend's wife was an exceptional woman, and he
was very fond of Lady Dawlish. He had often envied
Percy his happy home life, but had so far failed to
find a lady he could admire as much as Merry
Dawlish, who laughed a lot and seemed to enjoy life

hugely in her own inimitable way. Even so, he *had*
felt something for Olivia, and he had certainly not
intended the tragedy that his carelessness had caused.
Indeed, it grieved him that she had been put in such
a position, for without fortune and friends to stand by
her, she was ruined.

So what was he going to do about it? Having just
returned from the country, he had little inclination to
return there—and to Northamptonshire! Nothing interesting ever happened in such places.

Harry's besetting sin was that he was easily bored.
Indeed, he was often plagued by a soul-destroying
tedium, which had come upon him when his father's
death forced him to give up the army life he had
enjoyed for a brief period, and return to care for his
estates. He was a good master and did not neglect his
land or his people, but he was aware of something
missing in his life.

He preferred living in town, where he was more
likely to find stimulating company, and would not
have minded so much if Olivia had gone to Bath or
Brighton, but this village…what was it called? Ah
yes, Abbot Giles. It was bound to be full of dull-
witted gentry and lusty country wenches.

Harry's eye did not brighten at the thought of
buxom wenches. He was famed for his taste in cy-
prians, and the mistresses he had kept whenever it
suited him had always possessed their full measure of
both beauty and wit. He believed the one thing that
had prevented him from giving his whole heart to
Olivia was that she did not seem to share his love of

the ridiculous. She had found some of his remarks either hurtful or bewildering. Harry thought wistfully that it would be pleasant to have a woman by one's side who could give as good as she got, who wasn't afraid to stand up to him.

'What an odd character you are to be sure,' Harry told his reflection. It was a severe fault in him that he could not long be pleased by beautiful young women, unless they were also amusing.

Harry frowned at his own thoughts. It was not as if he were hiding some secret tragedy. His mother was still living, and the sweetest creature alive—but she had not been in love with his father, nor his father with her. Both had carried on separate lives, taking and discarding lovers without hurting the other. Indeed, they had been the best of friends. Harry believed he must be like his mother, who seemed not to treat anything seriously, and was besides being the sweetest, the most provoking of females.

No matter! He was a man of his word. He had given his word to Olivia, and the fact that she had jilted him made no difference. He must go after her, try to persuade her that he was not so very terrible. As his wife, she would be readmitted to the society that had cast her off—and that surely must be better than the fate which awaited her now.

'Beckett…' he called, making up his mind suddenly. 'Put up a change of clothing for me. I am going out of town for a few days.'

'Yes, milord,' said his valet, coming in. 'May one inquire where we are going?'

'You are going nowhere,' Harry replied with an odd little smile. 'And if anyone asks, you have no idea where I am...'

'Come in, dearest,' Beatrice said, meeting her sister at the door. It was some six days since she had received Olivia's letter, and her heart was pained by the look of tiredness and near despair in Olivia's face. Oh, that rogue, Ravensden! He should be hung, drawn and quartered for what he had done. 'You look cold, my love. Was the journey very tiresome?'

The road from London to Northampton was good, and could be covered easily enough in a day, but the country roads which led to Abbot Giles were far from ideal. Olivia had travelled down by one of the public coaching routes the previous day, and had been forced to find another conveyance in Northampton to bring her on. All she had been able to hire was an obliging carter, who had offered to take both her and her baggage for the sum of three shillings. A journey which must have shaken her almost rigid! And must also have been terrifying to a girl who had previously travelled in a well-sprung carriage with servants to care for her every whim.

How could the Burtons have sent her all this way alone? Anything might have happened to Olivia. It was as if her adoptive parents had abandoned all care for her along with their responsibility. The very least they might have done was to send her home in a carriage! Their heartlessness made Beatrice boil with anger, but she forced herself to be calm. It did not matter now! Her sister was here and safe, though desperately weary.

'Beatrice…' Olivia's voice almost broke. Clearly she had been wondering what her reception would be, and Beatrice's concerned greeting had almost overset her. 'I am so very sorry to bring this trouble on you.'

'Trouble? What trouble?' Beatrice asked. 'It is with the greatest pleasure that I welcome my sister to this house. We love you, Olivia. You could never be a trouble to me or your family…' She smiled and kissed Olivia's cheek. 'Come and meet Aunt Nan, dearest. Our father is busy at the moment. We try not to disturb him when he is working, but you will meet him later. He has asked me to tell you how pleased he is to have you home again.'

At this the sweet, innocent face of Miss Olivia crumpled, the tears spilling out of her bright blue eyes.

'Oh, how kind you are,' she said, fumbling for her kerchief in the reticule she carried on her wrist. She was fashionably dressed, though her pelisse was sadly splashed with mud, and the three trunks of personal belongings she had brought with her on the carter's wagon would seem to indicate that the Burtons had not cast her out without a rag to her back. 'I know you must think me wicked…or at the very least foolish.'

'I think nothing of the kind,' Beatrice said, leading her into the tiny back parlour, in which a welcoming fire was burning. It was usually not lit until the evening, neither Beatrice nor her aunt having time to sit much during the day, but this was a special occasion, and the logs they were using had been a gift from Jaffrey House, sent down specially by their very wealthy and illustrious neighbour the Earl of Yardley.

The Earl had a daughter named Sophia by his second marriage, of whom Beatrice imagined he was fond. The girl was near Olivia's own age, and very striking, with black hair and bright eyes. Beatrice knew her of course, though they seldom met in a social way.

Mr Roade did not often entertain, nor did he accept many invitations, but the Earl's family were seen about the village, and Beatrice was sufficiently well acquainted with Lady Sophia to stop and speak for a few minutes whenever they met. She thought now that it was a pity her father had turned down some of the kind invitations the Earl had sent them over the years. It would have been nice for Olivia to have made a friend of Sophia Cleeve.

'My dear Olivia,' Nan said, bustling in. She was wearing a mob cap over her light brown hair, and a dusting apron protected her serviceable gown. 'Forgive me for not being here to greet you. I was upstairs turning out the bedrooms. We have only the one maid, besides the kitchen wench, and it would be unfair to expect poor Lily to do everything herself.'

Olivia looked amazed at the idea of her aunt having been busy working in the bedrooms, then recollected herself, blushed and seemed awkward as she went forward to kiss Nan's cheek.

'Forgive me,' she said. 'I fear I have caused extra work for you.'

'Well, yes, I must admit that you have,' Nan said, never one to hide the truth. 'However, I dare say the room needed a good turn-out—it was your mother's, you know, and has not…'

'Nan doesn't mean that you are a bother to us,' Beatrice said as she saw her sister's quick flush. 'The room you have been given was our mother's private sitting-room, not her bedroom—that is where she died, of course, and I felt it might distress you to sleep there.'

'I was about to tell Olivia that,' Nan said. 'We've been waiting for the bed to arrive—it was ordered from Northampton, but arrived only this morning on the carter's wagon. Had we not needed to wait, your room would have been ready days ago.'

'It was time we had a new bed,' Beatrice said smoothly, with a quick frown at her aunt. 'The one we have in the guest room, which is at the back of the house and depressingly dark, is broken in the struts which support the mattress. It is still there, of course, though since no one ever comes to stay, it does not matter…'

'I see I have caused a great deal of trouble,' Olivia said. 'You have been put to considerable expense on my account.'

'Nothing of the sort,' replied Beatrice. 'Take off your bonnet and pelisse, dearest. I shall ring for tea—unless you would like to go straight up to your room?'

Olivia looked as if she would dearly like to escape, but forced herself to smile at them.

'Tea would be very nice,' she said. 'I have a few guineas left out of the allowance my…Lord Burton made me earlier in the season, but I did not care to waste them on refreshments at the inns we passed. Besides, I was in a hurry to reach you. I shall give you what money I have, Beatrice, and you may use it for expenses as you see fit.'

'Well, as to that, we shall see how we go on,' Beatrice said, and reached for the bell.

It was answered so promptly that she imagined Lily had been hovering outside in the hall—a habit her mistress disliked but not sufficiently to dismiss her. Like Bellows, Lily did not complain if her wages were late, though Beatrice paid the girl herself, and usually on time.

'Tea please, Lily.' She turned to her sister as the maid went out again. 'That's right, dearest, sit by the fire and you will soon feel better. We shall talk properly later. For now, I want you to tell me all the news from London…that is, if you can bear to? We hear so little here, you know, except when neighbours return from a visit to town.'

'You know of course that the Prince was declared Regent earlier this year?' Olivia looked at her doubtfully.

'Yes, dearest. Papa takes *The Times*. I am aware that trade has been bad, because of Napoleon's blockade of Europe, and that unemployment is high. I didn't mean that sort of news…a little gossip perhaps, something that is setting the Ton by its ears?'

. Olivia gave a little giggle, her face losing some of its strain.

'Oh, that sort of news…what can I tell you? Oh yes, apart from all the usual scandals, there is something rather exciting going on at the moment…'

She had taken off her outer clothing now, revealing a pretty travelling-gown of green velvet.

'There is a new French modiste in town. She is the protégée of Madame Marie-Anne Coulanges, who was herself once apprenticed to Rose Bertin—who, you must know, was a favourite dressmaker to Queen Marie Antoinette.' Olivia paused for effect. 'They say Madame Coulanges was once a friend of Madame Félice's mama, and that is why she has taken her up—anyway, she presented her to her clients, and Madame Félice has taken the town by storm.'

Beatrice smiled as she saw the glow in her sister's eyes. Her little ruse had worked, and Olivia had lost her shyness.

'How old is Madame Félice?'

'Oh, not more than two-and-twenty at the most, I would think. She has pretty, pale hair, but she keeps it hidden beneath a rather fetching cap most of the time, and her eyes are a greenish blue. I think she might be beautiful if she dressed in gowns as elegant as those she makes for her clientele, but of course it would not be correct for her to do so. Though no one really knows much about her…she is something of a mystery.'

'How exciting. Tell me, dearest, is she very clever at making gowns?'

'Oh, yes, very. Everyone, simply everyone, is dying to get their hands on at least one of her gowns—but she is particular about who she dresses. Would you believe it? I heard she actually turned down the Marchioness of Rossminster, because she had no style! She will dress only those women she thinks can carry off her fabulous gowns. Of course they are the most beautiful clothes you have ever seen. No one can touch her for elegance and quality.' Olivia dropped her gaze. 'She was very nice to me. I have one of her gowns and she was to have made a part of my wedding trousseau...' Her cheeks fired up as she spoke. 'I have the gown she made for me in my trunks. I will show it to you later, if you wish?'

'I would like very much to see it,' Beatrice said. 'If it is as smart as the one you are wearing...it must be lovely.'

She had been about to say that her sister would have little opportunity to wear her beautiful clothes now, but bit the words back before she was so cruel as to remind Olivia of all that she had lost.

'We shall talk of other things later,' she said. 'There is much to talk about, Olivia—but we have time enough.'

'Yes,' Olivia said, losing the sparkle she had gained when telling her sister the news about Madame Félice. 'Of course, London is thin of company now. I believe the Regent is to leave London for Brighton at the end of this month... Oh, that is today, isn't it?'

Her mouth drooped as though she were remembering that she would no longer be a part of the extravagant set that surrounded the Prince Regent and privileged society. However, the arrival of the tea-tray and the delicious cakes that Beatrice had spent the morning baking brought her out of the doldrums a little.

'These are delightful,' she said, choosing from the pretty silver cake-basket and chewing a small, nutty biscuit. 'Quite as good as anything I have tasted anywhere.'

'Beatrice made those for you herself,' Nan said. 'They are Bosworth Jumbles, but Beatrice adds her own special ingredients to the recipe, which some say was picked up on the battlefield at Bosworth in 1485, hence its name. Your sister will make some lucky gentleman an excellent wife one day.'

'Did you really make them?' Olivia stared at her. 'You are so clever. I have never cooked anything in my life.'

'I can teach you if you like, and there is a very good manual by Mrs Rundle, called *Domestic Cookery*,' Beatrice said. 'I know it may seem tedious at first, Olivia, but living in the country has its compensations. We have nut trees and fruit from our own orchards, berries from the kitchen gardens, and we make our own jams and preserves. It can be a rewarding way to pass the time.'

'Yes, of course.' Olivia lifted her head, as though wanting to show she was not above such things. 'Yes, I am sure I shall soon settle in…'

Chapter Three

Beatrice took her sister up to her room half an hour later. She had offered to help her unpack her trunks, being reasonably certain that Olivia had never had to do so for herself before. Olivia had accepted and was now showing her some of the lovely clothes she had brought with her.

'These are only a few of my gowns,' she told Beatrice. 'I left some of the more elaborate ones behind. I shall scarcely need the gown I wore to be presented to the Regent at my coming out…or most of my ballgowns. Lady Burton did say she would send them on…' Olivia blinked rapidly to stave off the tears gathering in her eyes. 'She was kinder than Lord Burton…she said she would be prepared to forgive me, but that he was adamant the connection must be cut.'

'Well, perhaps he will relent in time…'

'No.' Olivia's lovely face was pale but proud. 'I do not wish to return to their house…ever. What I did was right, and I shall not grovel to be forgiven.'

The subject was dropped, for Beatrice did not like to see her sister so upset. Instead, she exclaimed over the gowns they were unpacking, especially the one made by Madame Félice, the extraordinary French modiste who had suddenly arrived in town some months earlier.

'It is very lovely,' she said, holding it against herself. The jewel green of the fine silk actually became Beatrice very well, setting off the colour of her hair, and was, of course, far more stylish than anything she had ever made for herself. 'No wonder everyone is so anxious to order from her—but does no one know where she worked before she came to London? Was it in Paris?'

'No one seems to know anything about her before she set up her shop…but they whisper that she is the mistress of a very rich man.'

'Oh, why do they say that?' Beatrice looked at her curiously.

'They say she brought money to Madame Coulanges's salon. It stands to reason. She must have a protector—where else would she get the money to set herself up in a fashionable establishment? If she had no money, she would be desperate to take any order…'

'Yes, I see the reasoning behind such gossip,' Beatrice replied. She frowned. Her education had been to say the least unusual, and her opinions were strong in such matters. 'But I do not see that the money must have come from a protector. Why cannot a woman be successful for herself, without the aid of a man? Why must everyone always assume the worst? There could be other reasons why she was able to bring money to Madame Coulanges. Perhaps she inherited some from a wealthy relative, and used it to set herself up in business. She might even have won it in a game of cards.'

'It is intriguing, isn't it?' Olivia said. 'I dare say her story will come out eventually—and that will set the tongues wagging again. For the moment, she can do no wrong—no one would think the worse of her for having a wealthy protector. She does not mix in society, other than to dress her wealthy clientele, of course, and could never hope to marry into a good family.'

'Alas, I fear you are right. We are all too much governed by convention. I am sure we shall hear more in time,' Beatrice said. 'The news may be slow in filtering through to the four villages, but it arrives in due course.'

'The four villages...' Olivia stared at her in bewilderment. 'I am not sure what you mean?'

Beatrice laughed. 'Oh, I am so used to that way of speaking of our neighbours. I mean the villages that lie to the north, south, east and west of Steepwood Abbey, of course: Abbot Quincey, which is really almost a small market town these days, Steep Abbot and Steep Ride...which is tiny and remote, and lies to the south of the Abbey—and our own.'

'Oh, yes, the Abbey. We passed by its outer walls on our journey here. Is life affected much by what goes on there?'

Once again, Beatrice laughed. 'We have a wicked Marquis all our own,' she said. 'The stories about him would take me all night to relate, but I will only say that I cannot vouch for any of them, since I have scarcely met him—except for the night he almost knocked me down as he rushed past on his horse, of course.'

'That was very rude of him,' Olivia said. 'If he is so unpleasant I do not wonder that you do not care to know him.'

'No one cares to know the Marquis of Sywell—except perhaps the Earl of Yardley. I am not sure, but I think there is some story about them having belonged to the same wild set years ago, before either of them had come into their titles. It was a long time ago, of course. Before the old Earl, who was the seventh to bear the title, I believe, banished his son to France, lost the Abbey, which had been in his family for generations…since the middle of the sixteenth century…to the present owner, and then killed himself.'

'Indeed?' Olivia looked intrigued. 'Why was the son banished? Oh, pray do tell me, Beatrice—was it because of a love affair?'

'Have you heard the story?'

Olivia shook her head. 'No, but I should like to if it is romantic…to die for love is so—so…'

'Foolish,' Beatrice supplied dryly. 'Perch on the window-seat, Olivia, and I will sit here on this stool. It is a long story and must be explained properly or you will become confused with all the different Earls and not know who I mean.'

Olivia nodded, her face alight with eagerness. For the first time since her arrival, she seemed truly to have forgotten her unfortunate situation. Beatrice took heart, determined to make her story as interesting and entertaining as she could for her sister's sake.

'Well, the present Earl of Yardley, the eighth if I am right, was not born to inherit the title or the estate. His name when this story begins was Thomas Cleeve, and his family was no more than a minor branch of the Yardleys. It was then that he and his cousin (the last Earl before this one: I told you it was complicated!), some folk say, were both members of the rather loose set to which Lord George Ormiston belonged—he, to make things plain, is our wicked Marquis of today.'

'Yes, I see. He is now the Marquis of Sywell and he owns the Abbey,' Olivia said. 'Please do go on.'

'Lucinda Beattie, the spinster sister of Matthew Beattie, who was our previous vicar and died in…oh, I think it was eleven years ago…told our mother that Thomas Cleeve was disappointed in love as a young man and went off to India to make his fortune. That part was undoubtedly true, for he returned a very wealthy man. I know that he married twice and returned a widower in 1790 with his four children (twin boys of fourteen years, Lady Sophia, who I dare say you will meet, and his elder son, Marcus). He built Jaffrey House on some land he bought from his

cousin Edmund, then the seventh Earl of Yardley...
Are you following me?'

'Yes, of course. What happened to the romantic
Earl?' Olivia asked, impatient for Beatrice to begin
his tale. 'Why did he banish his son—and what was
his son called?'

'His son was Rupert, Lord Angmering, and I believe *he* was very romantic,' Beatrice said with a
smile. 'He went off to do the Grand Tour, and met a
young Frenchwoman, with whom he fell desperately
in love. It was in the autumn of 1790, I understand,
that he returned and informed his father he meant to
marry her. When the Earl forbade it on pain of dis-
inheritance, because she was a Catholic, he chose
love—and was subsequently banished to France.'

Olivia was entranced, her eyes glowing. 'What
happened—did he marry his true love?'

'No one really knows for certain. Some of the older
villagers say he would definitely have done so, for he
was above all else a man of honour, others doubt
it...but nothing can be proved, for the unfortunate
Lord Angmering was killed in the bread riots in
France...'

'Oh the poor man—to be thrown off by his father...' Olivia's cheeks were flushed as the similarity
to her own story struck her. 'But you said his father
killed himself?'

'As I have heard it told, the Earl was broken-
hearted, and when the confirmation of his son's death
reached him in 1793, he went up to town, got terribly
drunk and lost everything he owned to his friend the

Marquis of Sywell at the card tables. Afterwards, he called for the Marquis's duelling pistols and before anyone knew what he intended, shot himself—in front of the Marquis and his butler—the same one who remains in Sywell's employ today.'

'It was sad end to his story, but it had a kind of poetic justice—do you not think so?' Olivia asked. 'He blamed himself for the loss of his son and threw away all that had been precious to him...'

'It may be romantic to you,' Beatrice replied with a naughty look, 'but it meant that the people of the four villages have had to put up with the wicked Marquis ever since. And according to local legend, there was a time when no woman was safe from him. He has been accused of all kinds of terrible things...including taking part in pagan rites, which may or may not have involved him and his friends in cavorting naked in the woods. Some people say the men wore animal masks on their heads and chased their...women, who were naturally not the kind you or I would ever choose to know.'

'No? Surely not? You are funning me!' Olivia laughed delightedly as her sister shook her head and assured her every word was true. 'It sounds positively gothic—like one of those popular novels that has everyone laughing in public and terrified in private.'

'Dear Mrs Radcliffe.' Beatrice smiled. '*The Mysteries of Udolpho* was quite my favourite. How amusing her stories are to be sure. What you say is right, Olivia...but it is not quite as funny when you have to live near such a disreputable man.'

Olivia nodded. 'No, I suppose it would be uncomfortable. Tell me, did the present Earl inherit his title from the one who banished his son and killed himself?'

'Yes. After the death of the Earl and his son Lord Angmering there was no one else left—or at least, if Rupert left an heir no one has heard of him to this very day.' Beatrice shook her head. 'No, I am very sure there was no child. An exhaustive search was made at the time, I have no doubt, and no record of a marriage or a child was found. Had it not been so, the title could not legally have passed to Thomas Cleeve, and it was all done according to the laws of England, I am very sure.'

Olivia nodded, acknowledging the truth of this. 'Besides, even if Lord Angmering had by some chance had a son…what would there be for him to inherit if his grandfather had lost all his money gambling?'

'Nothing in law, I suppose. You may be certain, had there been an heir, he would have come forward long ago, to claim his title and anything that might still belong to his family.'

'I suppose so…' Olivia was reluctant to let her romantic notion go, and smiled at her sister. 'That was a fascinating story. I wish someone would come back to the villages and declare himself Lord Angmering's son, don't you?'

Beatrice threw back her head and laughed heartily. 'I should never have told you—you will be expecting something to happen, and I do assure you it will not.

No, my dearest sister, I must disappoint you. I think the Earl of Yardley is secure in his title—and since his fortune is his own, he does not need to prove anything.'

'No, of course not.' Olivia stood up and went to embrace her sister. 'Thank you for telling me that story—and thank you for taking me in with such kindness.'

'You are my sister. I have always loved you. I would not have wished for you to be in such circumstances—but I am happy to have you living here with us.' Beatrice looked at her intently. 'You have not regretted your decision to jilt Lord Ravensden?'

'I regret that I was deceived into accepting him,' Olivia replied, 'but I do not regret telling him that I would not marry him.'

'What did he say to you?'

'I—I wrote to him,' Olivia said, her cheeks pink. 'I could not have faced him, Beatrice. I was so…angry.'

'What made you change your mind about marrying him, dearest?'

'I was told by a rather spiteful girl…a girl I had hitherto thought of as my friend…that Ravensden was marrying me only to oblige Lord Burton, that he wanted me only as a brood mare, because he desperately needs an heir. He is past his green days, and no doubt imagined I should be grateful for the offer…'

'He could not have been so cold-blooded?' Beatrice was shocked. 'My dearest sister! I believe you have had a fortunate escape. Had you not learned of his callousness before your wedding, you would have been condemned to a life of misery at this brute's hands.'

Olivia took her hands eagerly. 'You do understand my feelings,' she cried, her lovely eyes glowing. 'I was afraid you would think me capricious—but when I realised what he had done...I realised I could not love him. In fact, I saw that I had been misled by his charm and his compliments.'

'His charm?' Beatrice frowned. How could this be? It did not equate with the monster she had pictured. 'Was he so very charming?'

'Oh, yes, I suppose so. Everyone thought so...but I found his humour a little harsh. Though of course he was toadied to by almost everyone because of his wealth, and the Regent thinks him a great wit.'

'It seems to me the man was eaten up by his own conceit,' said Beatrice, who had never met him in her life. 'I see what it was—you were the catch of the Season and Burton's heir. He wanted the fortune...'

'But most of it will be his anyway,' Olivia said, frowning. 'That is what is so particularly cruel. He had no need to oblige his cousin. Why propose to me if he did not care for me in the least?'

Beatrice saw that her sister was not so indifferent as she pretended. Whether it was her heart or her pride that was most affected, it was equally painful for her.

'Well, we shall talk of this again,' she said. 'Do not distress yourself, dearest. You will have no need to meet Lord Ravensden again, so you may forget him. One thing is certain, he will not dare to follow you here...'

Beatrice spent a restless night dreaming of disinherited heirs, pagan orgies and—inexplicably!—a man being boiled in oil. She woke early, feeling tired and uneasy. Which served her right for spending a great deal of the evening recounting stories of the wicked Marquis, making them as lurid as possible for her sister—who was clearly of a romantic disposition.

Had Olivia been other than she was, she might have settled for the comfort marriage to Lord Ravensden could provide, but she could not help her nature, and Beatrice could not but think she had made the right decision.

'Let me but get my hands on that creature,' muttered Beatrice.

Oh, he should pay, he should pay!

Olivia was certainly trying to settle to her new life, and had so far been very brave, but it was bound to be hard for her. They must all do whatever they could to lift her spirits in the coming months.

Such were Beatrice's thoughts as she left her father's house that morning, the day after her sister's arrival. It was the beginning of November now and a little misty. Mindful of the cold, she had wrapped up well in her old grey cloak, which was long past its best.

She had decided to visit the vicarage, her intention to ask the Reverend Edward Hartwell and his wife to dine with them the next week. She would also send a message to Ghislaine, and beg her to come if she could. It was the best she could offer Olivia by way of entertainment, though obviously not what she was accustomed to… The sound of hooves pounding on the hard ground gave her a little start.

She paused, watching as horse and rider came towards her at a gentle canter. This was not the bruising rider who had almost knocked her down a week ago, but a stranger. She had never seen this gentleman in Abbot Giles or any of the four villages.

His clothes proclaimed him a man of fashion, even though he was dressed simply for riding. As he came nearer, she could see that he looked rather attractive, even handsome, his features striking. He had a straight nose, a firm, square chin, and what she thought must be called a noble bearing.

Beatrice realised the rider was stopping. He swept off his hat to her, revealing hair as thick and glossy as it was dark—almost as black as a raven's wing. He wore it short, brushed carelessly forward in an artfully artless way that gave him a dashing air. He might have come straight from the pages of Sir Walter Scott's poems, some noble creature of ancient lineage.

'Good morning, ma'am,' the stranger said, giving her a smile that was at the same time both sweet and unnerving in that it seemed to challenge. 'I wonder if I could trouble you to ask for directions? I have lost my way in the mist.'

'Of course. If I can help, sir.' Beatrice glanced up into his eyes. So startlingly blue that she was mesmerised. Goodness! What a remarkable man he was to be sure. 'Are you looking for somewhere in particular?'

'I do not know the name of the house,' he replied. 'But I am looking for the Roade family of Abbot Giles…Miss Olivia Roade Burton in particular.'

An icy chill gripped Beatrice's heart. Surely it was not possible? She had been so sure that Lord Ravensden would not dare to come here. Yet who else could it be? This man was handsome, his smile charming—and *now* she looked at him properly, she could see that he was arrogant, too sure of himself and proud. A despicable man. Indeed, she wondered that she had not noticed it immediately.

Why had he come here? Beatrice's mind was racing frantically. If this was truly Olivia's jilted suitor, he must not be allowed to take her sister by surprise.

'Ah yes,' she said. 'I do know of the family—but I fear you are travelling in the wrong direction.'

'Is this not the village of Abbot Giles?'

'Has Ben turned the milestones round again? It really is too bad of him!' Beatrice said in a rallying tone. 'He will do it, poor foolish fellow. It all comes from the bang on the head, but it is most confusing for visitors.'

'Pray tell me,' the stranger said, a gleam in those devastating blue eyes. 'How did poor Ben come to receive such a damaging blow to the head?'

'It is a long story,' Beatrice said hastily. She pointed to the open gates of the Abbey grounds. 'If you follow that road, the narrow lane there, then keep on past the lake and turn to your right near the ruined chapel, you will come to the village in time.'

'That sounds a little complicated…'

'It is a short cut, any other route would take you miles out of your way.'

'I see, then I shall follow your instructions. Thank you, ma'am.'

The stranger looked at her hard for a moment, then set out in the direction she had indicated. Beatrice waited until he had been swallowed up by the mist, then turned on her heel and ran back to her home.

The visit to the Reverend Hartwell could wait. Olivia must be alerted to the fact that her abominable fiancé had come in search of her!

Beatrice found her sister at breakfast. A few pertinent questions confirmed her suspicions—no two men could have such blue eyes!

'I fear Lord Ravensden has come in search of you,' she told the startled and disbelieving Olivia. 'I managed to send him on a fool's errand—but he will find his way here before long.'

'I shall not receive him!'

'I do not see how you can refuse,' Nan said, frowning at both sisters. 'Beatrice, it was very wrong of you to misdirect his lordship. If he has come all this way to see your sister, he must be hoping to repair the breach between them.' Her gaze rested on the agitated Olivia. 'Are you sure you were not misled by the spiteful tongue of a jealous rival? Is it not possible that your fiancé has some real regard for you?'

Olivia was silent, then said, 'I do not think it

can be so, aunt. And even if it were…I have realised that my own feelings were mistaken. I cannot marry him.'

'For the sake of decency you should at least receive him.'

Olivia looked at her sister. 'Must I, Beatrice?'

Beatrice had had time to reflect. 'I think perhaps Nan is right. It will be awkward for you, dearest, but a few minutes should suffice—and Nan will stay with you.'

'Will you not be with me, Beatrice?'

'I think it best if Lord Ravensden does not see me,' Beatrice said, feeling slightly guilty now. Olivia's ex-fiancé must have ridden hard to reach the village so soon after her departure, and she had added an unnecessary detour to his journey. 'Be brave, dearest. Be dignified, and positive—and then you need never see him again.'

'Where are you going?' Olivia asked as she turned to leave.

'To complete my errand,' Beatrice replied. 'I must be swift. It would not do for Lord Ravensden to see me when he calls.'

She laughed, turned and walked quickly out of the house. Lord Ravensden was going to be very angry when he discovered the trick that had been played on him, and indeed he had every right. It would be much better if he never learned that the woman who had sent him on a wild goose chase was sister to the one he sought!

*   *   *

'Now what game might she be playing?' murmured Lord Ravensden to himself. 'Do my instincts serve me right, or have my wits been addled by the mist?'

Harry had the oddest feeling that the woman he had met a few minutes earlier had deliberately sent him in the wrong direction. Her story had been plausible, but somehow he had not quite believed in the village idiot who had a habit of turning milestones so that the arrow pointed the wrong way—dashed heavy things, milestones! Yet why should a young woman— and one who looked reasonably sane!—go out of her way to deceive him?

He had previously enquired the way of a man who could, in the politest terms, only be called a country bumpkin. The fellow had rambled on in some unintelligible tongue so that Harry had begun to wonder if he had inadvertently crossed the channel in the night, leaving him none the wiser as to his whereabouts. He had seen no signs of any kind for miles on end, and had been on the point of knocking at a house in the village he had just passed, when he had seen the young woman walking towards him through the mist.

She had looked to be gently born. Somewhat plainly dressed perhaps, but not without a pleasing air. He had judged her to be the wife of an impoverished squire—or perhaps the parson, since she seemed to be heading in the direction of the church he had passed some way back. Her speech had been soft, cultured, gentle on the ear. He had followed her directions, because he could not see why such a woman should lie to him.

Some ten minutes or so later, he was beginning to think he should have followed his instincts and continued straight ahead. It was difficult to get his bearings in this damned mist. He appeared to be following a narrow track, little more than a footpath, and on private land by the looks of it—that dark shape in the distance must surely be the Abbey that lay at the heart of the four villages. He was just considering whether or not he should turn back when he saw someone coming towards him.

The gentleman, for he was surely that, though carelessly dressed, was wearing a shabby black cloak which flapped in the wind. His hair was thinning at the temples—he wore no hat despite the inclement weather—and perched on the end of his nose was a pair of gold-rimmed spectacles.

'Good morning, sir,' Harry called. 'May I have a moment of your time?'

'Why certainly, sir,' replied Beatrice's father. 'We do not often have strangers in our village. Are you by chance lost? The rare visitors we do get often become confused about the four villages—which one do you seek?'

'Abbot Giles. I am seeking the Roade family. I am Lord Ravensden, and Miss Olivia Roade Burton is my fiancée. I am trying to find her.'

'Are you indeed? Well, now, what a fortunate chance that you should come this way.' Mr Roade beamed at him. He recalled Beatrice telling him something about her sister's fiancé but could not re-member the precise details. No matter, it was plain enough what he ought to have known. 'You've come to stay, of course. Olivia will be delighted to see you. Not sure where we shall put you—but Beatrice will think of something. She is nothing if not resource-ful.'

'Beatrice?' Harry was beginning to think all the inhabitants of this place were stark, raving mad. 'She is…?'

'Of course, we haven't met. How remiss of me.' Mr Roade reached up to offer his hand to Lord Ravensden, who had to bend down to take it from his position high on his horse's back. 'Bertram Roade. Olivia is my youngest daughter…'

'…and Beatrice presumably the elder?' An appre-ciative glint entered the blue eyes. 'Touché, Beatrice!' Harry was no slow top and he knew at once why he had been sent off in the wrong direction.

He dismounted, beginning to walk at Mr Roade's rather fast pace. It seemed his host was in a hurry to reach his home.

'You won't mind if I hand you over to the ladies once we reach the house?' Mr Roade asked. 'It came to me this morning, you see. I often see things more clearly when I'm out for an early walk…something about the air. Now I need to get back and work. I forget otherwise. If I don't put my ideas on paper as soon as they come, they slip away. It is most unfor-tunate.'

'Yes, I do see…' Many things were becoming clear

to Harry. 'Would you care to tell me about this idea, sir? Between us, we might remember it.'

'Capital notion! Beatrice thought of it, but she had it wrong, this time. She is a great help to me, excellent mind, you know. Let the steam pass through, was what she said—but it has to be the water itself. Beatrice wasn't thinking properly. I dare say she was worrying about having guests. Women do, don't they? We aren't used to entertaining. My fault, of course. I've let things slide since my wife died. Loved her, too much.'

'Yes, I understand,' Harry said, observing the deep sadness in his companion's mild eyes. 'But you were telling me about your idea...'

'Ah yes,' Mr Roade brightened. 'It will be pleasant to have a guest in the house again. Especially a man of sense. You've come to marry Beatrice, haven't you?'

'Olivia, sir,' Harry replied, eyes gleaming. The imp of mischief was sitting on his shoulder. 'Unless you would prefer me to marry Miss Roade, of course?'

'No, no, I remember now, it was Olivia. Mind you, Beatrice would make any man an excellent wife— very good at economy. Don't understand it myself. Trouble is, I'm not sure I could spare her. Looks after me too well, besides being an excellent companion.'

'Make sure any prospective suitor is as rich as Midas,' Harry suggested with an air of innocence. He was enjoying himself hugely. Indeed, he did not recall a time when he had been so well entertained. Had he really thought Northamptonshire would be boring? So far it was proving to be vastly diverting.

'Why do you say that?' Mr Roade looked at him, suddenly intent.

'Your son-in-law would then have a house large enough to accommodate Miss Roade, and any other member of her family she cared to bring with her.'

Mr Roade seemed struck by this. 'What I need,' he confided, 'is someone who would be willing to let me try out my ideas for gravity heating.'

'Gravity heating?' Harry's brows rose. 'What a very good notion! Yes, I do see the possibility. Very useful in old houses—if it could be made to work.'

Beatrice's father beamed at him. 'Exactly. It will make life so very much more comfortable. There have been some problems with overheating, you see—but I shall work them out in time. I suppose you do not happen to have an old and very draughty house?'

Harry chuckled. 'My dear Mr Roade,' he said. 'As it happens, I have far too many of them…'

Beatrice said goodbye to her friends and set off on the road home again. She had spent a good hour sipping Mrs Hartwell's rose cordial, and chatting about the gossip in the villages.

Mrs Hartwell had told her that her husband was worried about the stories of lights being seen in Giles Wood again.

'Edward fears that some kind of unpleasantness is going on there,' she said. 'I do hope he won't take it upon himself to investigate.'

'No, indeed,' Beatrice said. 'It might be dangerous.'

'I have tried to tell him,' the anxious wife said with

a sigh. 'But he feels it is his duty to his parishioners to keep an eye on such things…'

'Yes, of course,' Beatrice agreed. 'It must be a worry to him.'

The Reverend Hartwell had come into the parlour at that moment. He had been pleased to see Beatrice, who led the exemplary life he thought suitable for a spinster of her advanced age. At three and twenty, she would no doubt devote her life to her father, as was right and proper in the circumstances, and no more than her duty. He spoke kindly of her sister and promised they would all dine together the next Thursday. He had also promised to send his groom over to Steep Abbot with a note for Mademoiselle de Champlain, and to provide a bed in his house for her afterwards so that she need not walk all the way back to Steep Abbot on a cold, dark night.

'For I could not rest easy in my mind if the young lady were forced to go near the Abbey grounds after dusk, Miss Roade. There is no telling what might happen to any woman foolish enough to venture there alone.'

Beatrice agreed, feeling glad that he had no idea she had done so herself a few days previously. She took her leave of her kind friends, and set out to walk back to her home, which was at the outskirts of the village.

The mist had cleared now. Beatrice thought that Lord Ravensden must have found his way to Roade House long since, spoken with Olivia, taken his dismissal like any gentleman and gone. Presumably he would already be on his journey back to Northampton.

She entered the house by way of the kitchen, calling for her aunt. Nan was not in her usual place at the table. Beatrice and Nan did all the cooking for the household, though the kitchen wench, Ida, prepared the vegetables. *She* was sitting by the fire, warming her feet—which always had chilblains in the winter—and peeling potatoes for the mutton stew they were to have that evening. Since the mutton was likely to be old and tough, being the cheapest Beatrice could buy, it would need a long, slow cooking over the fire to make it tender.

'Have you seen my aunt, Ida?'

Ida wrinkled her brow and thought about it, then her face brightened as inspiration came.

'No, Miss Beatrice—not since her went off in a fluster, be an hour ago nigh on I reckon. There be a gentleman caller...'

Beatrice nodded. Good, that meant their unwelcome visitor had found his way here—she had felt a little guilty after she had sent him off in the wrong direction—but she had wanted to prepare Olivia. She was sure Lord Ravensden would have spoken to her sister and departed by now.

'Where is Mrs Willow at the moment?'

'I think her went upstairs, miss. Her and Lily both.'

'And my sister?'

'In her room, miss. Her's locked herself in an' won't come out never no more!'

'That is rather dramatic of her,' Beatrice said, hiding her smile. It appeared that more had been going on here than she had expected. 'I shall go and find my aunt and see what is happening.'

Ida's version of events was not to be trusted, since the girl was sometimes more than a little confused in her thinking. It was doubtful that anyone else in the villages would have employed her, but she worked for little more than her keep and was useful for the rough work in the kitchen. Besides, Beatrice had felt sorry for her when she came asking for work and looking as thin as a piece of thread that might snap in two. She did not look that way now, for Beatrice fed her servants on the same fare she offered to her family.

She would try the parlour first, Beatrice decided, since she could see no reason why both Nan and Lily should be required to tidy the bedrooms.

'I'm back…' The words died on Beatrice's lips as she opened the door and walked into the parlour. A fire had been lit, but only recently, and had barely caught hold. A man was kneeling before it, using the bellows in an effort to persuade the flames to rise. 'Good grief…'

The man turned to look at her, his blue eyes narrowing as he saw who was standing there. 'Miss Roade, I presume,' he said. 'Tell me, is it the custom in Abbot Giles to freeze your visitors to death? This damned fire does nothing but smoke and will not catch.'

'It will do so in a moment,' Beatrice said, 'but like the one in my bedchamber it does tend to smoke when the wind is in the wrong direction. Papa will invent something to stop it one day, but until then we can do nothing but endure.' She frowned, wondering why she was telling him this. 'Indeed *you* need not endure it, sir. I am surprised you have not already begun your journey back to London. You must know that you have no business in this house?'

'I am aware of no such thing,' Harry replied, his usual good humour unusually dented. He was cold and tired, and no one had offered him refreshments. His fiancée was in her bedroom, refusing to see him, and he was starving. 'I was invited to stay by Mr Roade—and I may tell you that I have every intention of doing so. At least until Olivia consents to see me. I have not come all this way to be sent off like a puppy with my tail between my legs.'

'Had you not destroyed my sister, you need not have come, sir. And as for leaving, Lord Ravensden, you would be well advised to do so at once. For I am told my sister will not see you. If you return to Northampton, you could find a decent inn where the chimney does not smoke.'

'You have already tried to be rid of me,' Harry said, glaring at her. 'Did you hope that I would lose myself completely and be found in some isolated wasteland frozen to the ground—or just that I would grow tired of wandering and take myself off?'

'I am sure I do not know what you mean,' Beatrice said untruthfully. 'Had you kept on the way I directed you and turned to the right by the chapel, the footpath would have led you back the way you had first gone, and you would eventually have come to the village.'

'Eventually, no doubt. Always providing that I did not freeze to death in the meantime.' He sneezed, as if to prove that there was a distinct possibility that he might have done so. 'At least, someone might have the decency to offer me a glass of wine.'

'Has no one done so?' Beatrice felt her cheeks grow warm. She was normally the most hospitable of women, and willing to share whatever she had with her guests. 'I shall attend to it myself, sir. We do not have a choice to offer you—but my father's sherry is tolerable.'

'Thank you,' Harry replied, eyes narrowing. She looked younger than he had thought when they met in the lane, and her cheeks had a becoming colour. Despite her drab gown, she had a natural elegance and was attractive in her own way. 'Oh, dash it, Miss Roade, need we be at outs with one another? This is an awkward situation, and some way must be found to set things right.'

'You owe my sister an apology!'

'Indeed, I do, Miss Roade. If she would but come out of her bedroom, I would make it—and then perhaps we could begin to sort this mess out.'

'You should have gone at once to Lord Burton, confessed that it was all your fault, and asked him to reinstate Olivia.'

'I was out of town. As soon as I returned, I went to see him. The fool is as stubborn as a mule. He declares that he will only forgive her if she marries me.'

'Oh…' Beatrice was at a stand. His answers were reasonable, and seemed to indicate he knew himself at fault—but clearly this was put on for her benefit. She remembered the tale that had been told to Olivia. The man was a rogue! 'You wretched man! How could you have been so careless as to say in public that my poor sister was fit only for a breeding mare?'

'No!' Harry was outraged. 'Dash it all! I shall not be accused of such a coarse remark. I may have mentioned it was not a love match to a friend…but the rest is simply a lie, added on by a malicious tongue.'

'And you expect me to believe that?' She glared at him, daring him to make another excuse.

'My dear Miss Roade,' fumed Harry. 'I neither know nor care what you may believe at this precise moment. I have been frozen half to death, left alone in an icy parlour with a smoking fire and no refreshment—and I am hungry. I meant to beg Olivia to reconsider, but now I am wondering if that would be wise. Obviously, her family are all quite mad—or I have partaken of bad wine and fallen into a nightmare from which I shall awake with a monstrous headache.'

Beatrice stared at him. Had he tried to ingratiate himself with her, she would have thought him a charlatan. Now she was torn between righteous anger and amusement, finding herself hard put not to smile.

'Indeed, you have been cruelly treated, sir,' she said in a softer tone. 'I do assure you that you have

not been drinking bad wine, at least to my knowledge,
for my father can afford so little wine that he buys
only the best. Besides, as you have not been offered
any, I cannot see that the opportunity was there. As
to whether we are all a little mad in this household…well, you must decide that for yourself. I shall
go at once to fetch sherry wine, bread and cheese. I
fear I can provide nothing more until we dine, unless
you would prefer almond comfits and a raspberry
wine my aunt makes herself?' She saw his expression
of disgust and was betrayed into a laugh. 'Do be
seated, Lord Ravensden. I shall not let you go hungry
for much longer.'

She left him staring after her and went back to the
kitchen. There was bread freshly baked by Nan that
morning, a good local cheese, pickles—and a decent
sherry. No matter what else they lacked, Beatrice
never let her father go without his sherry. They also
had a few cases of good table wine in the cellar,
bought in better times, and brought out on the rare
occasions when they had dinner guests, but she was
not about to open a bottle for Lord Ravensden. No,
indeed! He could have sherry and ale, some bread and
cheese—then he could take himself off back to
London, where he belonged.

'Ah, there you are,' Nan said, coming down the
stairs as Beatrice emerged from the kitchen with her
tray. 'Oh dear, I should have seen to that. I quite
forgot. I was upstairs, trying to persuade your sister
to come down.'

'Pray take this to the parlour,' Beatrice said. 'The

fire may have caught by now and Lord Ravensden will be able to eat in peace. I shall go up to Olivia and see if she will come out for me.'

'She says she shall stay there until he leaves.'

'And he says he will not leave until he has seen her.'

Nan shook her head at such obstinacy and took the tray from Beatrice, who ran up the stairs and knocked at her sister's door.

'Olivia dearest, pray let me in.'

'Has he gone?'

'He is in the parlour having some bread and cheese. He wants to apologise to you.'

'I do not want to hear him. Ask him to go away.'

'He will not leave until you see him. He is the most tiresome creature ever. I do not wonder that you refused to marry him. Indeed, I should think you foolish if you did…'

There was a sound that might have been a laugh or a sob, then Olivia unlocked her door. She was pale and strained, but had not been crying. She pulled a wry face at her sister.

'Lord Ravensden led Papa to believe we are still to marry. He has invited him to stay—and he will. I know he will! Believe me, Beatrice, he will not be moved. He has the oddest notion of humour. He seems amused by this whole situation—at least, he was laughing when Papa brought him home.'

'He was not laughing when I left him. Do not worry, Olivia, I do not believe he will stay long. A man like that…he will find this house uncomfortable.'

'Yes, I dare say,' said Olivia, who was finding her own bedroom, where the fire had not been lit, less than cosy. 'Must I truly see him, Beatrice?'

'I think you must at least grant him a hearing. I believe he means to beg your pardon—and ask you to reconsider…'

'I do not want to marry him.'

'Nor would any woman of sense,' Beatrice said, 'though it seems he may not have said all the things you were told—but you need not fear, dearest. If after you have listened, you still do not wish to marry him, I shall support you. He may stay tonight, if he insists, then go back to town tomorrow.'

'And you will not try to make me marry him?'

'Is that what Lord Burton did?' Olivia nodded, and Beatrice felt anger at the foolish manner in which her sister's adoptive father had behaved. 'That was indeed bad of Lord Burton. Well, I shall not do any such thing. Wash your face and tidy yourself. I shall do the same, then we will go down together and beard the lion in his den. The sooner we set him to rights, the sooner he will leave us.'

'Yes.' Olivia looked slightly ashamed. 'It upset me to see him laughing with Papa. It was as if he were making game of me—but I dare say they were talking of something else.'

'Yes, I am certain they were. Papa would not laugh at you, dearest—and I do not believe Lord Ravensden would either, for all he is the most provoking creature.'

Beatrice smiled at her and went away to tidy herself.

Downstairs in the parlour, Harry had persuaded Mrs Willow to stay and drink a glass of sherry with him.

'Forgive me,' Nan said as he began to eat with a hunger that showed he was much in need of his breakfast. 'I should have offered food and wine. I was so startled by Olivia's foolish behaviour that it went right out of my mind.'

'Pray do not apologise, ma'am,' Harry said. 'I should have stopped to break my fast at an inn, but I was in a hurry to reach this house. All this trouble has been a dreadful misunderstanding.'

'I was sure it must have been,' Nan replied, smiling at him. 'I dare say it was no more than the spiteful wagging of a malicious tongue.'

'More than one, I fear,' Harry admitted. 'And my fault. I was away at the time it began. Had I been in town, much of this could have been avoided...'

'I knew it could not be as Olivia thought.' Nan looked at him with approval. He was in her opinion a very charming man, and in coming down at once to set things right had behaved in a proper manner. Olivia would be a fool not to take the opportunity he was offering her. 'I am sure my niece will see sense when you have talked to her...' She broke off as voices in the hall announced the arrival of Beatrice and Olivia. 'I must leave you now, sir. I have many tasks awaiting me.'

She rose to her feet as her nieces entered together,

their arms linked, then nodded to him, and smiled at the sisters in passing as she went out.

Harry was already on his feet. Olivia was looking pale and nervous. He was acutely conscious of his part in her distress. What a villain Burton was to behave so ill towards her!

'Forgive me, Miss Olivia,' he said at once. 'I startled you by arriving so suddenly. Yet I felt it was necessary to follow as soon as I returned to town and learned what had happened in my absence.'

'I was...upset,' Olivia said, her head going up proudly. 'But I should not have run away. It was good of you to come, sir, but there was really no need to put yourself to so much trouble. My decision was final. I fear you have had a wasted journey.'

Harry glanced at Beatrice, who had gone to the fire and seemed to be attacking the logs with a poker.

'Will you not at least allow me to apologise? My remarks were careless, but you have been told lies. I said only that it was not a love match. The rest has been added by another.'

'Surely that is enough?' Olivia said, her eyes meeting and challenging his bravely. 'Had I not believed you cared for me...'

'Oh, but I do...' Beatrice attacked the logs so fiercely that Harry could only think she was wishing it was him she was wielding her weapon against. 'I have a high regard for you, Miss Olivia. I am not a believer in romantic love, but I think we might have made each other tolerably happy. Indeed, I still believe it. It is my earnest wish to set things straight between us.'

There was a crackling sound behind him and then a great whoosh. Suddenly, the flames began to shoot up the chimney, throwing some warmth into the room at last.

'That is very much better,' Beatrice said with some satisfaction. She got to her feet, dusting her hands and brushing at her skirt. 'I think you should accept Lord Ravensden's apology, Olivia. Then he may go back to London and be at peace with himself.'

'Yes, of course,' Olivia said and smiled at him. She really was remarkably pretty when she smiled. 'I believe that you may have been misquoted—but it makes not the slightest difference...'

He moved towards her, reaching out to take her hand, but she stepped back, hiding her hands behind her back.

'Will you not at least try to forgive me?' Harry asked. 'Lord Burton has told me he will not relent towards you unless we marry... I never wished to bring you harm, Olivia.'

'But you have done so,' Beatrice said when Olivia was silent. 'My sister is too distressed to think clearly now. I pray you, sir, let her be. You have put your case, give her time to consider. If she should change her mind, she may write to you.'

'No,' Olivia said, her manner nervous but determined. 'I shall not deceive you, sir. I have discovered that we shall not suit. I was mistaken in my feelings.

Time will not make me change my mind. My answer will always be the same.'

'At least let me...' Harry sneezed three times in quick succession. 'Damn! Excuse me, ladies, but I fear I may have taken a chill.' He glared at Beatrice as though it were her fault. 'It must have been that wretched mist earlier. It was damp and chilled me to the bone.'

She stared him down. 'I shall make you a hot posset and then you may be on your way. If you leave at once, I dare say you might be home in time to sleep in your own bed.'

'Leaving? Surely not,' said Mr Roade, entering the room at that moment. 'Beatrice, what can you be thinking of? Ravensden has come to visit me. Asked him meself. Wanted you to see, Ravensden—I've started on the new drawings we discussed earlier. Come and have a look, give me your opinion, there's a good fellow.'

'Yes, of course, sir, delighted.' Harry inclined his head to the frustrated Beatrice. 'Excuse me, Miss Roade, Miss Olivia.' An odd smile flickered about his lips as he followed his host from the parlour.

Olivia looked at her sister in exasperation. 'You see—he won't go. He will keep on and on asking me to marry him until I say yes.'

'Is that what he did before?'

'Yes...though just in a teasing way so that I was not always sure he really meant it. I believe he thought I would keep on saying no. He was surprised when I finally accepted him.'

'Surely not?' Beatrice frowned. 'I would not have thought it of him. He seems genuinely to regret what happened. Do you not think you might reconsider…?'

'Please do not try to change my mind. You promised you would not, Beatrice.'

'And I shall not—if you are certain? You do realise that you may never get another chance to marry well? If you stay here with us, you may never marry at all.'

Olivia lifted her chin proudly. 'I do not wish to marry without love. I would rather take a post as a governess!'

Beatrice hid her smile. There was little chance of Olivia finding such a situation. She was far too pretty. Very few women would want to take her into their households in any position.

'Well, I dare say it will not come to that,' she said, and glanced out of the parlour window. 'It looks as if the fog has come down again. We cannot force Lord Ravensden to leave until that clears, which, by the look of it, will not be before the morning.'

Olivia glanced out of the window and pulled a face. 'Let us hope it has cleared by the morning. Perhaps he will realise the situation is hopeless and leave by then.'

'I am sure one night in our guest room will make Lord Ravensden eager to be on his way,' Beatrice said, a quiver of laughter about her mouth. 'I believe I did tell you that the bed has a broken support…'

Chapter Four

Harry heard the mattress strain ominously beneath him as he turned restlessly. The damned thing sagged in the middle! He had never been so uncomfortable in his life. If this was another of Miss Roade's stratagems to get rid of him... He groaned as he felt the ache in his limbs. It was not just the bed. He could not remember ever having felt this ill in his life. He was hot and cold by turns, his head going round and round.

'Mad...must be mad...mad to come to such a place...'

And still his feverish thoughts would not let him be! Having seen the obvious poverty in which the Roade family lived, Harry knew his conscience would never let him abandon Olivia to her fate. Somehow he must persuade her to marry him, and if he could not...it was a thorny problem, made more difficult by the fact that both the Roade sisters were damnably proud!

Yet he had brought this situation about, and somehow he must resolve it. He did not know why the look of accusation in Miss Roade's eyes pricked at him so much, but he could not seem to get her face out of his mind.

'Go away, woman,' he muttered feverishly. 'Let me be, will you?'

He would think of something…something that would ensure Olivia and her family did not suffer for his carelessness. If only the room would stay still for long enough for him to think properly! He groaned, searching for a comfortable spot in the bed and finding none.

He was ill, and must fetch help. Harry tried to struggle from the bed but found it too much for his spinning head, and fell back against the pillows with yet another groan.

Next door in her own room, Beatrice heard the moaning and frowned. Really, there was no need to make such a fuss! She imagined that the bed was a little uncomfortable, but it was his own fault. If he had not been so careless…*anyone can speak thoughtlessly*. The thought flashed into her mind unbidden.

Beatrice had soon realised that Lord Ravensden was not the monster she had imagined him on reading her sister's letter. He had been thoughtless and a little cruel, but perhaps he had not meant to be. She believed he was sincere in his wish to make amends.

Olivia seemed adamant that she would not have him, but only a few days had passed since Lord Burton had thrown her out. How would she feel when she began to miss her friends, and the balls she had found so delightful? She was trying to be brave, but Beatrice believed she must cry sometimes when she was alone. How could it be otherwise?

Hearing more groans, Beatrice frowned and put her pillow over her head. The man was impossible! Had he no consideration for other people? This was a small house, the bedrooms close to one another. If he kept this up, she would never sleep. She only hoped that one night in their guest room would ensure his early departure in the morning.

'Oh, Beatrice,' Nan said, coming in before she was properly awake the next morning. 'I am so sorry to disturb you, my love—but I think we shall have to send for Dr Pettifer. Lily went in to take Lord Ravensden's hot water this morning, and she says he was raving, quite out of his mind. I went at once to see for myself, and I fear she is right. The poor man has a nasty fever.'

'A fever—you mean he is ill?' Beatrice's conscience smote her. If their guest was ill, it was her fault. She had sent him out of his way in the mist, then he had been left in an icy parlour—and the guest room had not been used in years! Lily had lit the fire and put a warming pan to the mattress, of course, but it could not have been properly aired. 'I shall come at once.'

She slipped a dressing-robe over her nightgown, ran out into the hall and entered the next room without knocking. One look at Lord Ravensden's flushed face told her that Nan was right. He was ill. Very ill, by the way he tossed and turned restlessly. She walked over to him, laying her hand on his forehead.

'You poor man,' she said, as she found it hot and damp. 'What an unfeeling wretch I am to have let you suffer.' She looked at Nan with remorse. 'I heard him groaning during the night and imagined it was because of the bed. You must send Bellows for Dr Pettifer immediately.'

'Yes, I shall do so at once.'

Nan hurried away. Beatrice gazed down at the sick man. There was no question of his leaving them now, not for several days. She had an obvious duty to care for him while he was ill.

'You provoking creature,' she said in the scolding but teasing tone she would have used had her dear papa been ill. 'If I was not certain that you are ill, I would think you had done this deliberately.'

'Don't cry, Mama,' Harry muttered, tossing restlessly on the pillows. 'Poor Lillibet's gone…still got me. She's gone to Heaven where all the angels…should have been me! Little angel…gone to be with…' A shudder took him and he started up, clutching at Beatrice's arm. 'It should have been me. Damn it! Do you hear?'

He was clearly wandering in his mind. Beatrice stroked the dark hair from his forehead. He was very hot!

'Yes, of course I hear, you foolish man. I dare say it should have been you if you are so certain of it,' said Beatrice in a soothing tone, wondering who

Lillibet was. 'Rest now, my dear sir, or you will be with the angels yourself very shortly.'

He seemed to relax as he heard the scolding note in her voice.

'Yes, Merry sweetheart. Always do as you say…'

He was delirious, and thought himself elsewhere. Beatrice went to fetch a cloth and a basin of cool water. She soaked her cloth, then returned to the bed and began to bathe his head, face and neck. As she pushed the covers back, she saw that he was not wearing a nightgown. He must be completely naked beneath the sheets! She recoiled in shock. What ought she to do now? She had never in her life been near a naked man before this.

Beatrice's thoughts raced as she took stock of her situation. What was she doing here alone in Lord Ravensden's bedchamber? She must be mad indeed! She ought not to be here—but who else would nurse him? Lily could not be trusted, and her aunt had too much to do. There was no choice. Beatrice could not turn her back on a guest when he was in need of help, particularly as she felt partially responsible for his illness. Besides, he was in no case to ravish her at this moment.

'Do you know the trouble you are causing me, you wretch? I dare say it matters not a jot to you that my reputation will be ruined if anyone ever learns of this?' Beatrice chuckled as she realised that in truth it did not much matter. She almost never went into society, and she did not wish to marry—or at least, she did not wish to marry anyone who had ever asked

her. 'The least you can do is to get better. I refuse to
be compromised by a man who gives up without a
fight. Do you hear me, sir? Die on me, and you will
lie uneasy in your grave, I promise you.'

'What are you doing?' Olivia had come to the door
in her dressing-robe. She entered cautiously. 'Is he
really ill? Not simply pretending so that he may stay
here longer?'

'Yes, I am afraid he is very ill,' Beatrice replied.
'I thought he was making a fuss last evening—for if
you remember, he sneezed several times during dinner. However, I was wrong. He has a fever and will
not be able to leave us for a while, dearest.'

'Well, I suppose it does not matter if he cannot
leave at once.' Olivia sighed. 'He is not really so very
bad, Beatrice. I liked him more than any other of my
suitors, which is why I took him in the end. I thought
I might come to love him, but I know now that I never
could. He has no real sensitivity, no depth of soul.
Ravensden finds everything amusing, and I did not
always see the point of his humour, which was an-
noying. I would rather he didn't die, though.' She
looked upset suddenly. 'Do you think this is my fault?
Is he dying of a broken heart because I jilted him?'

'I very much doubt it,' Beatrice said. 'He has
caught a chill, and it has turned to fever. I dare say
the room was damp. If anyone is to blame, it is me.
I should have let him take my bed and shared with
you. In fact, when the doctor comes, I shall ask him
if he can be moved to my room. He will be very much
more comfortable there.'

'He would not have taken the chill if he had not chased after me.' Olivia looked repentant. 'I ought to have forgiven him kindly, offered to be friends. I shall do so if he recovers.'

'When he recovers,' Beatrice said. 'I have no intention of allowing him to die in Papa's house. Whatever would people say? Now go away, Olivia. It is not fitting that you should be in his bedchamber.'

Olivia laughed. 'It is too late to worry over my reputation. Not that I should be of much use in the sickroom. I have never done anything useful in my life.'

'Then you may start now, my love,' Beatrice said with a smile for her sister. 'Ask Lily to help you change the linen on my bed, please. It must be fresh and clean, ready for Bellows to take our patient there once Dr Pettifer has been to visit him.'

She watched as Olivia left the room, then turned back to her patient. He was so very hot, threshing restlessly from side to side in his fever.

'You poor man,' she said in a softer tone than she had used earlier. 'I must think of something to ease you…'

'So sorry, Lillibet,' Ravensden's hoarse cry disturbed Beatrice as she sat dozing in the chair by the fire. 'I didn't mean to kill you…'

Beatrice felt the chill trickle down her spine. What had this man done that haunted him so? Was Lillibet another unfortunate young woman he had somehow driven to her death? As Olivia might have been had she been less brave.

She got up and went over to the bed. He was burning up again. She felt a shaft of fear. What must she do to save him? She could not just stand by and watch him die. Something deep within her cried out against it.

He had seemed a little easier when she had earlier bathed his face and neck, but he was clearly hot all over, thrashing wildly in an attempt to throw off the light cover which was all that covered his nakedness.

Bellows had put a nightgown on him when he was moved, but it had become soaked through within an hour and it had been removed again. The sheets had had to be changed several times, which was making a lot of work for Nan.

'You poor, poor man,' Beatrice murmured, her heart wrung with pity for his pain. She went to fetch her basin and began to bathe his face. 'Does that feel good, my dear?'

'Yes, Merry. So hot…so hot…'

Beatrice glanced at the door. It was the middle of the night. No one was likely to come near at this hour…but just in case… She went over to the door and locked it, then returned to the bed.

'Oh, well,' she muttered. 'I suppose I may as well be hanged for a sheep as a lamb.'

She took hold of the cover and peeled it back, revealing Lord Ravensden's naked body. For a moment she stared, fascinated by its perfection despite herself. This man clearly kept himself in prime condition.

She turned away, blushing at herself and her most unladylike thoughts, and went to fetch her basin. She rinsed the cloth out in cool water and began to sponge his chest and arms.

'If you dare to wake and realise what I am doing, I shall die of embarrassment,' she scolded. 'You really are the most tiresome man! I have no idea why I am risking my good name for your sake. I dare not even think what the Reverend Hartwell would say…'

Beatrice slipped her arm behind her patient, lifting him a little so that he could swallow. She pressed the spoon against his lips. He was at least more comfortable now, though he was still in the grip of the fever, still unaware of where he was and who was tending him.

'Open your mouth, you stubborn wretch,' Beatrice commanded. 'Do not imagine I have all day to waste. I have more important work waiting. There are the walnuts to pickle, and a sheet to mend. If you imagine you are more important than such tasks, you much mistake the matter. Papa will be most upset if there are no pickles at Christmas.'

'Scolding harpy…'

The moment his lips moved, Beatrice had the spoon inside and the bitter medicine slipped down his throat. He made a gagging sound, as well he might. She had tasted a drop and it was foul, but she believed it had done him good.

'Serves you right,' she said. 'Next time you will

think before you speak. Had you done so in the first place, we should none of us be in this situation.'

She laid her hand on his brow. He was much cooler now. This was the third day of his illness, and she had scarcely left his side, sleeping in the chair near the fireplace so that she could hear if he cried out. She was not sure if he was really aware of anything, but she had discovered that he usually responded if she scolded him.

Nan had remonstrated with her for spending so much time alone with him, warning her what others might think if it came out, but Beatrice refused to be moved. Her aunt was right, of course, but it was more important for the moment to save Lord Ravensden's life.

'No one but us need ever know,' she said. 'Besides, he must be properly cared for. Dr Pettifer said he could die…'

That prospect had frightened Beatrice so much that she had lavished care and attention on him, doing everything that needed to be done for his comfort herself.

She bathed his forehead again now. Unknown to anyone else, she had three times washed his naked body all over. He had been so hot, and the cool water had seemed to ease him, as had the balm she had rubbed into his back to ease the aching she knew he must be feeling—and of course his natural bodily functions had had to be attended.

Some young, unmarried women might have found the task beyond them, but Beatrice had taken it in her stride, thinking only of what her patient must be suffering.

She washed and dried his arms, neck, shoulders and face, marvelling at the firmness of rippling muscles. She had never imagined a man could be so beautiful. His skin was like polished satin, with just a light sprinkling of fine hair on his legs, chest and navel. She turned him over, washing and then massaging his back—such a strong back, with such smooth skin!

'I hope you won't remember all this,' she murmured as she settled the clean covers around him. 'If you do, I shall deny it. I shall say it was Nan—or that you imagined it.'

'Yes, Merry,' he murmured. 'That feels good... thank you. Sleep now...'

Who was the woman he called Merry? He had spoken to her several times in his fever. Perhaps she was his mistress? He was bound to have one, of course. Unmarried, a man in his thirties...oh yes, there must have been women.

What did she care? Beatrice frowned at her own thoughts. She was being very foolish. It could mean nothing to her if he kept a dozen mistresses—except for Olivia's sake, of course.

Nursing him and attending to his needs had brought her close to him, but that was something she must quickly forget. A man like Lord Ravensden was not for her. Even if he were not engaged to Olivia, which he was—or would be if Olivia would have him back. Besides, he was the most frustrating, stubborn creature on this earth, and scarcely worth the trouble she had lavished on him.

No, no, that was not true. Beatrice knew she had misjudged him at the beginning. He had tried immediately to do the right thing by Olivia, and that must excuse him much.

She had heard him tell Olivia that he had the highest regard for her. He wanted to marry her, and it would be better for Olivia if she could be brought to see the sense of the arrangement. Not a love match perhaps, but one that could bring respect and content on both sides. It was as much and more than was granted to most women.

Olivia had been upset over his carelessness, of course she had, but these past three days, she had shown a very proper concern for her ex-fiancé. She had carried trays upstairs for her sister, and tried very hard to help with some of the duties Beatrice was neglecting for Lord Ravensden's sake.

Was it possible that she was beginning to change her mind, to think that perhaps she might marry him? It would not be surprising when you thought of the alternative. Surely Olivia must see that she would be happier married to this man than living in a house where there was never enough money for the necessities of life, let alone the luxuries she had been accustomed to?

Any sensible woman must realise that, and Olivia was certainly not a fool, for all her romantic notions.

Lord Ravensden might be a stubborn, frustrating

creature, but he was not a monster. Indeed, given a chance, he might prove a comforting husband.

Beatrice looked down at her patient once more. He was sleeping peacefully now. She believed he had turned the corner. He would recover, though he must be given time to rest. There was no question of throwing him out until he was ready to leave.

The fever had broken at last. He would rest now—and he must never know that it was she who had tended him throughout his illness.

She would go to the room she now shared with her sister, and in the morning Lily could bring him some good nourishing broth.

The slight noise brought his eyes open. Harry's gaze moved towards the fireplace. A maid was putting logs on the fire. He felt a flicker of annoyance as he realised she must have woken him. Dash it all! It was barely light. What was the wench doing in his room? His manservant Beckett was usually so efficient, always careful not to wake him after a late night—and by the way his temples were throbbing, it must indeed have been a late night! He could not recall ever having woken with such a head. Whatever had he been drinking?

He closed his eyes against the nagging pain, opening them again as he sensed the girl hovering near.

'Where is Beckett?' he asked, a note of irritation in his voice. Had the girl not been properly trained? She ought not even to be in his room. What was his housekeeper thinking of to allow it? 'Dash it, girl, what are you doing here?'

'The mistress said I was to make up the fire, then bring you some nourishing broth if you were awake…'

'Mistress?' There was no mistress in his home! Where on earth was he? Harry struggled to remember. He must have drunk a devilish amount the previous night. Good lord! This wasn't his room. He had never seen it before. He tried to sit up, groaned and fell back against the pillows. 'Dash it, I'm as weak as a kitten!'

'You've been ill, sir. These past three days and more.'

'Ill, you say?' Harry stared at her in bewilderment. 'Have I, be damned?'

He tried to gather his thoughts. Vague memories began to filter into his mind. He seemed to recall something. Soft hands bathing him, easing the terrible throbbing aches in his back…a voice scolding him, but not in an unkind way. No, the voice had not been unkind, indeed, it had seemed to carry a hint of laughter, as though its owner was deliberately needling him, forcing him to respond, pulling him through his illness by the sheer force of her will. It must have been Merry Dawlish. He knew of no other woman who would do such intimate things for him.

'Fetch Lady Dawlish,' he said to the girl. 'Pray ask her if she will attend me here as soon as possible.'

The girl gaped at him as if he had said something

odd. What could be the matter with her? Merry did not usually employ half-wits.

'Who, sir?'

'Why, your mistress, of course.' Harry frowned as she continued to stare at him in that odd way. 'I would speak with her, thank her for her care of me.'

'Begging your pardon, sir. I don't know Lady Dawlish.'

'Don't know her—then where the hell am I?' Harry's brow furrowed as he searched for some elusive memory at the back of his mind. 'Who has been caring for…?'

'That will do, Lily,' a voice from the doorway said, and it was Harry's turn to gape as a vision of beauty appeared in his bedchamber. A woman with wild, curling hair loose about her face and shoulders was standing just inside the door. Dressed in a wrapping gown of some soft green material, clearly in the middle of her toilette, she looked none too pleased at having been disturbed. 'I had thought you were better, Lord Ravensden, but it appears you are still unwell.'

Harry blinked as he suddenly recognised her and the mists parted in his mind. Of course, he was in the house of Bertram Roade…but this was not the room he had been shown to that first night. He was very certain of that. And the woman standing at the foot of his bed, glaring at him as if she would like to take her poker to him, was surely not Miss Roade. She was a goddess, some celestial beauty newly sprung from the heavens.

'Where did you come from?' he asked, bewildered

by the transformation. This vision was not the slightly dowdy young woman who had sent him on a wild goose chase, nor the avenging sister who had wielded her poker to such good effect, but a warm, sensuous, lovely thing who stirred his senses.

Beatrice walked towards him, laying a hand on his brow. It was quite cool, and the fever had gone from his eyes.

'I dare say you feel a little strange this morning,' she said, frowning at him. 'You were very ill, sir. The fever has gone, but it may take a while for you to gather your wits.'

'You have certainly sent them flying,' Harry said, catching hold of her wrist as she would have moved away. 'I presume that I have you to thank for the nursing that has brought me through this damned sickness?'

'Me?' Beatrice had seen a gleam in his eyes that bothered her. Once before, a man had looked at her in that way. Goodness! Did Lord Ravensden imagine that because she had tended him in his fever she was a loose woman? 'No, indeed, sir, you much mistake the matter. I have scarce been in this room at all, except when the doctor called...' She noticed Lily still hovering in the doorway, her mouth open wide as if she were catching flies. 'You may go, Lily.'

'Yes, miss.' She hesitated still. 'His lordship's broth, miss—should I bring it now?'

'Yes, certainly.'

'No, she shall not,' Harry said at once. His head was beginning to clear now, though he still felt weak.

'Beef, that's what I want. Slices of rare beef, mustard and pickles.'

'It may be what you want, Lord Ravensden,' Beatrice said, making a silent note to send to Northampton for more supplies: such a guest was not to be fed on the stews, pies and bacon puddings that made up their usual diet. 'However, I can neither recommend nor supply it for the moment. My aunt has made a restorative mutton broth for you, and there is some cold ham and a pigeon pie for supper. If you are feeling well enough to stomach a little solid food by then, we shall be pleased to serve you, either here in your room or downstairs in the parlour.'

'It was you, wasn't it?' Harry's eyes narrowed. The scent of her was right, and that scolding note…she was the woman who had cared for him so tenderly. 'I have you to thank…for saving my life, I dare say.' Had he been taken ill at some wayside inn, he believed he might well be dead by now. Only the devotion and skill of this woman had got him through.

'No, indeed, you have not,' Beatrice said, lying calmly. 'My aunt tended you, sir. I have far too much to do to be waiting on sickbeds…and I must be about my business now.'

'Don't go,' Harry said, holding to her wrist with surprising tenacity for a man so weak. 'Please, stay a moment longer. I swear you are in no danger from me. I am as harmless as a new-born lamb.'

'Lily will bring your broth,' Beatrice said. She hesitated, yet knew she must not give into his pleading. Any intimacy between them must cease this instant.

'Or, if you prefer, my aunt will tend you, though she has much to do and can ill be spared. We do not have many servants in this house, my lord.'

'I am accustomed to a manservant,' Harry said. 'Can your father's man not attend me?'

'Bellows is not used to serving guests,' Beatrice said, her brow wrinkling. 'But…if you prefer it…'

'Let him come—unless you would like to feed and shave me yourself?'

The glint in his eyes unnerved Beatrice, and the touch of his hand was sending hot shivers through her entire body. She might almost have thought she had taken the fever from him! 'I believe Bellows will manage,' she said, thinking it would serve him right if the man nicked him. 'I shall send him up directly.'

'Thank you, you are very kind.' A wicked smile tugged at the corners of his mouth. 'You will please convey my thanks to your aunt, Miss Roade. Tell her I have never been so kindly treated in my life before, and I do thank her most sincerely for her care of me. For *all* her care…'

A bright flush stained Beatrice's cheeks. She turned her head aside, afraid that she was betraying herself. He knew! He was mocking her. Very gently, and his thanks were sincere—but that gleam in his eyes! It was not to be borne. Gentlemen did not look at respectable single ladies that way. She had stepped over the boundaries of proper behaviour, and she had better step back quickly or both her reputation and her peace of mind would be lost for ever. She pulled back, and this time he released his hold on her.

'I shall be glad to convey your message, sir. Nan will be pleased that you are feeling better this morning.' She frowned at him. 'I realise you are not up to the journey back to London just yet. We are unfortunately not used to visitors staying, but we shall do our best to make you comfortable—until you can leave.'

'I see you still wish to be rid of me,' Harry said. His eyes narrowed in thought. His wits must be addled! Why had he not realised before? Of course she dare not admit to having tended his sickbed; her reputation would be ruined if anyone guessed what she had done for him. And Harry was well aware of the extent of her services: he was dying to relieve himself this very moment! However, the barriers of convention were in place and he could not mention such an indelicate subject to the very proper Miss Roade. 'It is most unkind in you, Miss Roade. I am far too weak to even think of leaving for the moment.'

'No, of course you must not think of leaving,' Nan said, coming in at that moment with a tray. 'Not for several days, or however long it takes you to recover your full strength. We should not dream of it. Now, sir, I have brought you some good broth. I want you to eat it all and I shall not take no for an answer. Beatrice, my love, your papa needs you.'

'Lord Ravensden has requested that Bellows attend him,' Beatrice said, seizing her chance to escape. 'I dare say he will take some soup from your hand, Nan—since you have already done so much for him while he was in the fever. As for myself, I have far too much to do to waste time here…'

'Pickled walnuts…' Harry murmured, his eyes narrowed as a fragment of a woman's scolding flashed into his mind. 'Yes, I must not detain you further, Miss Roade. And I will gladly take the broth from you, Mrs Willow—but I would prefer Bellows to shave me, if you won't think it ungrateful of me.'

Beatrice left them together. She heard Nan laughing at something he had said as she went back to her own room to finish dressing. What had she been thinking of to rush to his room in her dressing-robe? It was only that on hearing the odd note in Lily's voice she had feared he was ill again…but what could it matter? Lord Ravensden was nothing but an inconvenience in the house. She had done her duty by him, but now he was over the worst and it would be as well for her if she were to stay out of his way until he left.

In the meantime she must send to Farmer Ekins, who, she believed, had killed a pig some days ago. The beef must come from Northampton, because she did not care to buy from the market in Abbot Quincey, where she believed the quality to be inferior, though they seldom bought such luxuries for themselves. Instead, they relied on poultry, mutton and pork bought from neighbouring farms.

Beatrice frowned as she thought of the dwindling supply of her housekeeping. It had taken money she could ill afford to pay, first for the new bed for Olivia, and then there were the doctor's visits to consider. He had called three times to see their patient; she did not grudge the money this would cost, of course, but it meant that she would have to find some other way to economise.

She did not want to take Olivia's few guineas if she could help it, but her own quarterly allowance was almost spent. Perhaps Papa…but there was the wine merchant to be paid, and they needed some more sea coals for the kitchen, besides wax candles for the parlour. It was truly vexing the way money just seemed to be eaten up by this house. She had often thought they might do better in a small cottage, but dear Papa could not bear to leave the home where he had once been so happy with his wife, of course.

Oh well, she would manage somehow. She had been putting a few shillings by to buy material for a new gown from Hammonds, the general store and linen draper in Abbot Quincey, but the purchase could wait. Her old gowns would do for a little longer.

She sighed as she looked at herself in the drab grey gown she was wearing that morning. It made her look so—so old and staid, and she didn't in the least feel like either of those things, but the dress was serviceable, and perhaps she could trim it with a new ribbon.

Dressed, her hair confined in a strict coil at the nape of her neck, only a few rogue curls allowed to escape about her face, Beatrice smoothed the skirt of her dress and went downstairs in search of her father.

He was in his study, working, in not the slightest need of her services. He did, however, look up at her entry, to enquire how their guest went on.

'How is Ravensden, m'dear? Better, I dare say, or you would not be here.'

'He is over the worst now, Papa, but he cannot leave us yet.'

'No, no, that would be unthinkable,' Mr Roade said. 'Besides, I like the fellow, Beatrice. Excellent mind. I think I shall go up and see him later, take some of my drawings to show him.'

'I am sure he will enjoy that, Papa,' Beatrice said, and smiled, at this marked measure of her father's approval. 'But you must not tire him. I believe he still feels a little weak.'

'Almost certainly,' her father replied. 'Foolish to travel in such inclement weather. Mist is very dangerous to the constitution, you know—damp and cold, the worst combination.'

'Yes…' Beatrice felt the guilt strike her. If it were not for her unkindness, Lord Ravensden might never have been taken ill.

'Very fortunate it happened here,' Mr Roade said. 'If he had been staying at an inn he might not have been so well looked after. You were exceptionally good to him, m'dear.'

'I did very little,' she said, her cheeks warm. 'If you do not need me, Papa, I have things to do.'

'Of course, of course…' He waved her away, but did not immediately return to the contemplation of his drawings when the door closed behind her. Mr Roade might be absent-minded, but he was not a fool. He knew well enough what kind of a life his daughter had been leading these past few years. 'Truly, a fine mind…very like your own, Beatrice…'

Chapter Five

'Where is Bellows?' Beatrice asked her aunt as she went into the kitchen the following morning. 'He is needed to bring in more logs for the parlour fire. Olivia is mending a sheet—and it is a little chilly in there. We do not want her going down with a fever.'

Nan glanced up from her work. 'Bellows was with his lordship earlier, then he went off on an errand— I believe he took Lord Ravensden's horse.'

'Goodness!' Beatrice said, looking startled. 'I hope he had permission.'

'I imagine his lordship wanted him to do something for him,' Nan said. 'They have been getting on like a house on fire. Bellows says it is quite like the old days. Apparently, he has shaved gentlemen before. It is only since Bertram lost most of his money that he began to do the outside work.'

'Yes, I suppose it is,' Beatrice said, frowning. There had been a time when things were not so very bad, before Sarah Roade died, her income from her family dying with her, and before Mr Roade had made so many unwise investments. 'Can Lord Ravensden not shave himself yet? Is he still feeling weak? Really, it is such a nuisance, but I dare say he does not realise how much we rely on Bellows. So thoughtless of him to send Bellows off on an errand. But what can you expect of such a man? It is all of a piece!'

'I dare say he is accustomed to being shaved by his man, and to having servants on hand to run his errands,' Nan said, looking at her thoughtfully. It was unusual for Beatrice to be so out of humour. 'I will ask Ida to bring in the logs. She is perfectly capable of doing it.'

'Yes, of course.' Beatrice sighed. 'I was just wondering.'

'Why do you not go up and speak to his lordship for a few minutes?' Nan asked. 'He enquired for you earlier, my dear.'

'I am far too busy,' Beatrice replied. 'We have guests for dinner on Thursday evening, Nan. Had you forgotten? I must do some cooking in preparation.'

'That is tomorrow,' Nan replied with a lift of her brows. 'Is there really anything you need to prepare today, my love?'

'I suppose not—but I ought not to visit Ravensden in his bedchamber,' Beatrice said, not quite meeting her searching gaze. 'I wonder that you should suggest it.'

'Ah…' Nan smiled as she saw the frustration in her niece's eyes. 'No, of course not. It would be immodest in you, and is not to be expected, since you scarcely went near his lordship the whole time he was so ill…'

'Pray do not tease me.' Beatrice gave a reluctant laugh. 'I had to tell him that, Nan. Only imagine what he would think if he knew it was I who had…well, I think it best that I do not go up. Papa said he was in high spirits when he saw him.'

'Just as you wish, dearest. Lord Ravensden did say that he might get up later today and come down…'

'The foolish man! He is not yet well enough.'

'I did tell him that he ought to stay where he was for another day at least, but he said…' Nan shook her head. Better not to repeat the exact words Lord Ravensden had uttered. He was here to persuade her youngest niece to marry him, not to seduce the elder. 'He said he did not care for lying abed, and that he was feeling very much better.'

'Well, I shall go and tidy our bedrooms,' Beatrice said. 'Lily can do Lord Ravensden's room later…'

She picked up her dusters and the lavender-scented polish, which had been made with beeswax from their own hives and lavender she had ground herself to extract the oil.

It really was most frustrating, Beatrice thought as she polished the chest of drawers in her father's room. Conventions were so foolish. Just because she was not married, she was barred from dropping into Lord Ravensden's bedchamber as her father did whenever he felt like it. As though she was in any danger of being seduced! Why, she did not even like him…if she did not think he would be a good catch for her sister, she would not have bothered for one moment whether he was ill or not.

He had come to them on Friday the first of November, it was now the sixth, only five days since he had been found ill. *Only five days?* Why did she care that he was foolish enough to be thinking of leaving his bed so soon?

To be sure, it did not matter! Why should she care what the tiresome creature did? Yet he had been so very ill the first three days, and she could not help wondering if he really was better now. No doubt the stubborn man would rise from his bed too soon, then take ill again on purpose!

Leaving her father's bedroom, she paused to dust a table in the hall. She was frowning, her thoughts far from comforting as she worked, and did not notice the man walking towards her along the landing, his boots making no noise on the old, worn carpet, until he was almost upon her.

'You really are busy, aren't you?' Harry said, making her jump and look round. 'I thought Mrs Willow was not telling me the truth when I asked her why you would not visit me—but it seems I was mistaken.'

'Lord Ravensden!' Beatrice cried, her heart leaping unaccountably. From fright, of course, nothing else. The wretched man had sneaked up on her! 'What are you doing up so soon? Surely you are not fit to come down yet? You would do much better to rest, sir.'

'If you will not come to me, I must come to you,' Harry said. 'I am much recovered, besides, I could not lie there another moment, knowing that I must be causing so much trouble to your household.'

'Indeed, you are not, you foolish creature,' Beatrice said. 'I did not nurse you to have you risk yourself so heedlessly…' She stopped, furious with herself for having been caught out. 'I meant my aunt, of course. It was Nan who nursed you.'

'Of course…' Harry's eyes gleamed. 'It would have been quite improper for you to have nursed me, Miss Roade. And, since you will not come near me now, I see that you are indeed a very proper young woman.'

'Not so young, sir. I am three-and-twenty, not a green girl to be doing anything so foolish as to—to…'

'…bathe a naked man?' Harry's grin was despicable. 'Massage his back when it was aching so very much?'

'Indeed, I should not dream of it,' Beatrice lied, her cheeks flaming. 'You must have dreamt it in your fever, sir.'

'Indeed, I must,' Harry agreed, his eyes warm and admiring. 'Forgive me, mistress, I fear I have a shocking sense of the ridiculous. It is very bad in me. Mama has always told me so, and Merry is forever scolding me for my wicked levity.'

'Who is Merry?' Beatrice's curiosity overcame her. 'You called for her so often…'

'Did I? I wonder why?' Harry frowned. 'She is the wife of Lord Dawlish, Percy Dawlish. He is my closest friend, and Merry has always made me welcome in her house. I believe I must have thought it was she who tended me so kindly.'

'Yes, I see.' Beatrice smiled, oddly content with his explanation. 'My aunt said you mentioned Merry by name several times.'

'Yes, *of course*, your aunt. A remarkable woman, Mrs Willow—in many ways.' Harry frowned as he saw her pick up her dusters. 'Do you always work so hard, Miss Roade? Or is it because I have upset your routine?'

'I do not mind a little polishing,' Beatrice said. 'Lily has taken on some of Bellows's duties for the moment, so I am doing her work this morning.'

'I see. It was thoughtless of me. I sent him into Northampton this morning, to run some errands for me. Forgive me, I should have asked if it was convenient before commandeering your servant.'

'You are used to a house filled with servants,' Beatrice said, a faint blush in her cheeks. 'This must seem a very odd establishment to you, Lord Ravensden. I apologise that we cannot offer you more in the way of comfort.'

'You have no need to apologise for anything,' Harry said. He took her hand. She was wearing a pair of old cotton gloves. 'So that is how you protect your skin. You have soft hands, Miss Roade. I am glad you take care of them. It would be a pity if they should be spoiled doing work more fitted to others.'

'I have become used to it,' she said, withdrawing her hand from his swiftly. 'Though I am more often baking than polishing. I enjoy baking and preserving…making my own healing balms and simples. Most countrywomen do, my lord.'

'Yes, I see.' Harry smiled at her, taking her breath away. 'And what else do you do when you are not thus employed?'

'I read…play Mama's pianoforte when I have the chance, and sew,' she replied. 'When the weather is better, I walk a lot.'

He nodded, his eyes intent on her face. 'You do not ride?'

'I used to before…' She stopped, dropping her gaze for fear he should see too much. 'It is expensive to keep a riding horse, Lord Ravensden. Papa borrows a mount from Mr Hartwell's stable now and then, and I suppose I might too—had I a decent habit that would fit me.'

'Ah…yes, I understand. Mr Roade told me that some of his experiments had proved costly in the past.'

'Yes…' Beatrice would not look at him. 'You must not pity us, my lord. We are content, Papa and I…it is poor Olivia that you should be thinking of.' Her eyes swept up to meet his, full of condemnation. 'It is she who has lost everything.'

'Yes, I realise that.' Harry's face assumed a serious expression. 'The problem is—what can be done about it?'

'You must persuade her it is in her best interests to marry you, of course.'

'Must I?' Harry's brows arched. 'Yes, I suspect that

would be the correct and proper course of action. Where may I find Miss Olivia at this moment?'

'She is in the parlour, mending a sheet.'

'Is she indeed? Poor Miss Olivia. I should go to her at once.'

'Yes, please do.'

Beatrice turned back to her polishing cloths as he inclined his head and walked past, but a muffled oath made her look round almost immediately, and she saw that he had halted, his hand clutching the banister rail as if he had needed support. She dropped her cloths and went to him at once, looking at him in concern.

'You, foolish, foolish creature,' she scolded. 'I might have known this would happen. I dare say you imagine that if you fall and half kill yourself, it will gain you a bed here for yet more days. Well, let me tell you, your stratagem will not work. Take my arm, sir, and we shall walk down the stairs together. I shall not have you ill again.'

'No, that would be very bad of me, wouldn't it? Since you have given up your room for my sake.' Harry's eyes danced with laughter. 'Unless you mean to send me back to that disgusting bed in your guest room now that I have recovered enough to be moved?'

'Oh, pray do not,' Beatrice said, smitten by guilt. 'I dare say it was all my fault you were ill, Lord Ravensden. The room had not been used in years, and though the fire was lit as soon as I understood your intention of staying, it could not have thoroughly aired the chamber.'

'I quite thought you meant to drive me out,' Harry said. 'That was a dashed uncomfortable mattress.'

'The struts are broken,' Beatrice said. 'I must ask Bellows if he can repair them.'

'So you do mean to banish me?'

'Be quiet, you provoking man,' Beatrice said as they reached the bottom of the stairs. 'Of course I do not mean to send you back there. I am quite comfortable sharing with my sister for the moment.'

'I understand there is a bedroom not in use…next to Mr Roade…' Harry raised his brows. 'If the bed were aired, I might move there in a day or so. Or is that bed also broken?'

'No, it is a very good mattress,' Beatrice said. 'It was my mother's room. She died in that bed, and it has not been used since. Obviously, I could not expect Olivia to sleep there, as it was where Mama died—but if it would not disturb you?'

'I have no fear of departed spirits,' Harry said. 'If Mrs Roade was as generous as her daughter, I am sure I shall sleep quite satisfactorily in her bed. And it would mean that you could be comfortable in your own room again.'

Beatrice kept her face averted. Really, such consideration from a man who was supposed to be careless! What did he hope to gain by this? Or was she being too critical?

'Well, I shall have the room aired properly since that too has not been used for a while, but you need not think of moving for a few days,' she said, then wrinkled her brow. 'Were you thinking of staying long?'

Harry gave a shout of laughter. 'You heartless minx,' he said. 'How can you think of sending me away, when I have been so thoughtful of your comfort?'

Beatrice glanced up at him, then quickly away as her heart raced. Really, the man had too much charm. He imagined it would gain him anything, but he much mistook the matter if he thought she was to be twisted around his finger.

'Pray go in to my sister,' she said. 'I am not so heartless that I would send you away before you have had a chance to win back Olivia's affections—but I must tell you that I shall not force her to take you, and nor will Papa. You must fight your own battle, sir.'

'Oh, indeed, I intend to do so, Miss Roade,' Harry said, a glint in his eyes. 'By whatever means necessary. They do say that everything is fair in love and war, do they not?'

Beatrice gave him a speaking look and left him, as he tapped at the parlour door and then went in. His manner left much to be desired in a prospective bridegroom, but she would not try to influence her sister one way or the other.

Had she been able to send him packing the first day, that would have been an end to the whole affair, but circumstances had been against her. Now they were all caught in the coils of a mischievous fate and must play out the game until its end.

It was Thursday the seventh of November. Beatrice was in the kitchen when Farmer Ekin's boy came in at the back door. She looked up, a flicker of amusement in her eyes, as he entered, basket on arm. It was immediately clear to her from his expression that he had news. Ned visited many of the houses in the four villages, taking produce from his father's farm to their customers, and he usually had some titbit of gossip to offer.

'There you be, Miss Roade,' Ned said, setting his basket on the table. 'A leg of pork, and two plump cockerels—for the gentleman as is stopping here, I dare say. Ma says there's no need to pay her. She don't want money, says she should rather have some of your good shortbread when you have the time to bake it, and a jar or two of your pickled walnuts. Pa is proper partial to them.' He grinned at her. 'His lordship's Miss Olivia's fiancé so they say...she be stopping, too, I reckon. A houseful, you've got, miss, and no mistake.'

'Well, as to the matter of Lord Ravensden being my sister's fiancé, we are not sure if they are suited or not. Nothing is yet settled,' Beatrice said. She offered him a plate of buns she had baked earlier. 'Have you any news for me, Ned?'

He parked his backside on the edge of her table, taking a bite of the bun and looking as if he appreciated it. Miss Roade's baking beat that of any cook in the four villages that Ned had come across, and she was always generous.

'Well, miss…funny you should ask that,' he said, a sparkle in his eyes. 'I was up at the Vicarage, see. Mrs Hartwell wanted some eggs and a side of bacon, but when I got there she was in the parlour, and our Mary told me…' He paused for effect. 'It seems the Vicar was up at the Abbey early this morning. Went to see the Marquis, on account of his thinking it was up to him to make him see the error of his ways…getting on a bit his lordship, and like to burn in the fiery pit for his sins, I shouldn't wonder.'

'Yes, I dare say you are right.' Ned's sister Mary was cook to the Reverend Hartwell's household. 'What happened? Was the Marquis very rude?' She imagined that he might be, and wondered that anyone should risk the kind of reception such a visit would be bound to bring on a chance caller.

'Our Mary says he opened the door hisself…the Marquis, that is, miss. In a flaming temper…drunk like as not, I dare swear.'

'Where was his butler?' Beatrice asked. 'Surely it is properly Mr Burneck's job to answer the bell?'

'Our Mary says she heard the Reverend telling her mistress. It was the Marquis what came to the door, still in his dressing-robe, and carrying on something awful he was 'cos the Crow hadn't been back to the Abbey all night. Went over to Northampton to see his cousin the previous afternoon and hadn't come back.'

'The Crow…'

Beatrice smiled at the name, one often used by the

village folk to describe Solomon Burneck, the
Marquis's butler. Burneck had been with his master
for years, even before the Marquis first came to the
Abbey. He was called the Crow because he always
wore the same rusty black clothes, and because his
nose was rather large and hooked like a bird's beak.
His eyes were narrow set, his lips thin and pale, but
despite his unfortunate looks, he was held in respect
and some awe by local people. Solomon Burneck was
a man of few words, but when he did speak it was
often to quote something from the Bible, and he was
thought to be a religious man. Why such a man
should remain in the employment of a master such as
the Marquis of Sywell was a mystery, but as Beatrice
knew well, there was no accounting for loyalty.

'I did not know Mr Burneck had any relatives.'

'She came with the Marquis, worked for him for a
few years,' replied the obliging Ned. 'You wouldn't
remember but Ma does; it were a good many years
ago when Mistress Burneck went off to be married…to a merchant with a house and shop of his
own, so me Ma told me.'

'And Mr Burneck has not yet returned from his
visit to his cousin? Well, that is odd,' Beatrice said.
'I wonder why he did not come back. Do you suppose
he has left the Marquis's employ?'

'If he has done a bunk, he ain't the only one,' Ned
said, hugely enjoying himself. 'The Marquis raved
and shouted at the Reverend something awful, told
him to clear off and never bother him no more—
and…' Ned paused importantly. 'He said as her la-

dyship had cleared off and left him. Said the whole place were empty 'cept for him. What do you think of that then?'

'The Marquis said his wife had gone…' Beatrice felt an unpleasant shiver trickle down her spine as her memory flashed back to the night she had nearly been knocked down by the Marquis's horse. That scream she had heard…that terrible, unearthly scream! 'How long ago did she leave?'

'Dunno…mebbe a few days, mebbe longer…' Ned shook his head. 'Our Mary didn't hear no more…the mistress come out of the parlour, caught her earwigging and sent her back to the kitchen.'

'And there were no other servants up at the Abbey at all?' Nan had come into the kitchen in time to hear the last part of Ned's story. 'Well, I suppose that is not surprising—after the way he has behaved in the past. I am sure no decent woman would dream of working there. No wonder folks say it is all going to rack and ruin. A crying shame, that's what I call it. He is an important landowner hereabouts. He ought to employ a lot of people, and I dare say there's suffering in the villages because of it. It is a great shame he ever came here!'

'It is all very odd,' Beatrice said. The cold chill settled at the nape of her neck. She could not help thinking about the blood-curdling scream she had heard the night she crossed the Abbey lands. 'Where do you suppose the Marchioness could have gone?'

'I dare say she has run off,' said the practical Nan. 'Who could blame her? Married to such a man, and with the house falling into ruin about her, as it must be.'

'Yes…' Beatrice nodded, but something was not quite right. She felt uneasy as she considered what might have happened to the Marquis's young wife. 'But…'

Nan shook her head as if in warning, and Beatrice remembered they were not alone. There was no need to spread gossip unnecessarily.

'Well, thank your mother for me,' Beatrice said. 'Tell her I shall bring the shortbread down this week-end…and perhaps you would like another bun to eat as you go?'

Ned grinned from ear to ear as he took the offering, then went out of the back door. His cheerful whistling could be heard as he sauntered off, carrying his empty basket.

'I know what you are thinking,' Nan said. 'But a still tongue makes a wise head, Beatrice. We must consider carefully. It would not do to start a malicious rumour only to have Lady Sywell turn up next week.'

'No, you are very right,' Beatrice said. 'Besides, Ned may have got it all wrong. I shall be interested to hear what the Reverend Hartwell has to say this evening and…' She broke off as the back door opened and Bellows entered, carrying a large wicker hamper.

'His lordship ordered this, Miss Roade,' her man-servant told her. 'There's a rib of beef, various cheeses and a whole ham, besides the wines and brandy waiting to be brought in from the carter's wagon.'

'And how are we supposed to pay for these things?' Beatrice felt her temper rising. 'There is no way we can afford luxuries like this...' She had opened the hamper to find jars of Gentlemen's Relish, marchpane comfits and candied fruits, also several pounds of tea and sugar—and chocolate! 'Really, it will all have to go back!'

'No need to take on so, miss,' Bellows said in his bluff way. 'It was all put on his lordship's account...same as the carriage and horses he ordered from the livery stables, together with the services of a groom and driver. Said it was easier to hire than send for his own...' Bellows faltered as he realised his mistress was now more incensed than ever. 'And various other things for his personal use...'

'How dare he?' Beatrice fumed. 'How dare he be so—so condescending as to think I would be pleased for him to pay for the food he eats in this house!'

She began to take off her apron. Nan eyed her warily.

'Where are you going, dearest? Not to remonstrate with his lordship, I hope? I dare say he meant it for the best...'

'Meant it for the best?' The light of battle was in Beatrice's eyes. 'It is an insult, Nan. And I mean to tell him so.'

'Do pray remember that the poor man has been ill...' Nan called after her as she walked from the kitchen. 'You do not want him to suffer a relapse.'

Beatrice was not listening. How dare Lord Ravensden insult her so? The only reason she had not offered him the beef he so urgently required was that she would not give him inferior meat, and for quality it was necessary to go into Northampton…to the superior establishment Bellows had clearly visited. Had he only been patient, she would have provided proper meals once she had been able to buy the provisions she needed.

Lord Ravensden was sitting in the parlour when she entered, a book of poems in his hand. He had obviously been reading to Olivia, for she sat idle, her mending laid down on the table beside her. She flushed and looked guilty as she reached for the shirt collar she had been turning for her papa.

'Lord Ravensden was reading aloud—*The Rime of the Ancient Mariner* by Mr Samuel Taylor Coleridge,' Olivia said, looking at her sister uncertainly. 'It is a favourite with me.'

'How very pleasant,' Beatrice said. 'Olivia, dearest—would you run upstairs and fetch my shawl, please?'

'Yes, of course…' Olivia seemed startled by something in her sister's tone, but rose obediently and left the room.

'Lord Ravensden,' Beatrice began as the door closed behind her. Her eyes flashed with green fire. 'I dare say you are not accustomed to staying at such a house as this one…'

Harry had risen to his feet at her entrance. He eyed her warily as he caught the note of anger in her voice. What had he done now?

'Forgive me, Miss Roade. In what way have I offended you?'

'You sent my servant to Northampton without a by your leave, then you have the effrontery to order food and wines—and to put them on your own account. I am aware that I have not been able to offer you the sort of hospitality you are accustomed to, sir, but had you been patient another day or so...'

'Forgive me,' Harry said in a contrite tone that somehow took her breath away. 'I have been clumsy and I see that I have hurt your pride. I meant only to ease the burden I know my visit must have thrust upon you. Indeed, I have no complaints at the hospitality I have received here. I doubt that anyone has ever offered me so much...'

Beatrice was not to be so easily mollified. 'You have sent for a carriage and horses—does that mean you intend to leave soon?'

'No, indeed, for I fear I could not yet contemplate a long journey,' Harry said and was taken by a fit of coughing, which lasted some seconds. When he had recovered enough, he went on, 'It was just that I thought it might be useful to have some of my own servants...to run my errands. And to help do the jobs that Bellows would normally do outside.'

'Oh...' Beatrice found herself at a stand. She could hardly complain when he had obviously been at pains to alleviate his reliance on Bellows's services. 'I see...well, I suppose that might be a help.'

'And you will forgive me?' Harry asked, a soft, persuasive note in his voice. 'Please accept my small

gift in the light in which it was offered, Miss Roade.
I understand you have guests this evening. Perhaps
you may find it of use for them if nothing else?'

'I dare say I may,' Beatrice replied and frowned at
him. 'You are a very tiresome creature, my lord.'

'Yes, indeed, I know it,' Harry said, and took a
step towards her. 'Miss Roade…'

Whatever he was about to say was lost as Olivia
returned with her sister's shawl. She looked relieved
to see that they had not yet come to blows.

'Is everything all right, Beatrice?'

'Yes…yes, of course.' Beatrice laughed, wondering why she had felt so very angry. 'It was all a mistake, I dare say.' She hesitated, then, 'We are to have
visitors this evening, as you know. Before they come,
I believe I ought to tell you both something I have
learned this morning…'

Olivia looked at her as she hesitated. 'Pray do go
on, sister. Have you some gossip to relate?'

'Well, yes, I have,' Beatrice replied. 'Do you recall
we spoke of the Marchioness of Sywell the evening
you arrived?'

'Yes, indeed…or at least, you said you knew nothing of her, that she was almost a recluse…'

'Well, it seems she has disappeared.'

'Disappeared?' Olivia stared at her, eyes opening
wide. 'What do you mean?'

Beatrice related the story as it had been told to her,
then drew her breath in sharply. 'You may remember
I was almost knocked down by the Marquis as he rode
past me one night…some two weeks ago now?'

Olivia nodded, her eyes beginning to glow with anticipation. 'Well, I had earlier heard the most terrible scream. I thought it must have been the cry of a trapped animal, but now…'

Olivia clapped her hand to her mouth. 'The poor Marchioness, she has been murdered by her wicked husband!'

'Well, as to that,' Beatrice said doubtfully. 'We should not jump to conclusions, Olivia…but it does seem a little odd.'

'How did the Marchioness's disappearance come to light?' Harry asked, the mischief beginning to dance in his eyes as he saw the gleam of excitement in Olivia's.

'The Reverend Hartwell made a visit to the Abbey,' Beatrice said. 'Mysterious lights have been seen at night in Giles Wood, and the Reverend Hartwell thought there might be some—some unpleasant things going on up there. It seems that he thought it his duty to remind the Marquis that he might be called upon to meet his Maker at any time and must repent his sins…'

'Of which there are many?' Harry asked, clearly enjoying himself. 'Tell me, what does he imagine is the significance of the lights? What has the Marquis been up to—surely not pagan orgies?'

Beatrice frowned at him in reproof. 'Well, you may not know of Sywell's reputation…but he has been denounced in the pulpit of every church in the county I dare swear. He is never sober, so they say…and no woman was safe from him, at least until he married.

She was much younger and very beautiful…though I do not recall ever having seen her myself. The adopted child of the Marquis's bailiff, she was educated by her stepmother, who was a governess—and she did not mix with the villagers nor go to school. She had been away from the village for some years, engaged in some trade, I suppose, but came back when her guardian died…and then the Marquis married her and carried her off to his home. After that, she has scarcely been seen again.'

'A very rogue!' Harry stated. 'It stands to reason— he must have done the dastardly deed.'

'Will you be serious, sir!' Beatrice gave him a speaking look from her wonderful eyes, which were themselves glowing like jewels. 'We do not yet know for certain that she is missing—nor that she has been murdered. She may have simply gone away for a visit.'

'If that were so, the Marquis would not have ranted of her absence to Mr Hartwell,' Olivia said. 'No, no, it is clear…he must have murdered her. And his anger at her disappearance was clearly to cover his own guilt. I am sure he has done away with her!'

'And buried her in the haunted chapel at dead of night,' said Harry helpfully. 'He must have got it from one of Fanny Burney's novels.'

'You rogue!' Beatrice cried, laughing at his tone. 'I liked *Evelina* excessively. Now if you had said dear Mrs Radcliffe…' Her eyes were bright with mischief. 'You have a wicked humour, sir. Why will you encourage Olivia in this nonsense?'

'How can you be sure it is nonsense?' Olivia asked. 'You did hear a scream—and you did see the Marquis rush past on his horse.'

'Yes…' Beatrice frowned. Olivia was more animated than she had been in days, her imagination clearly caught by the mystery of the young Lady Sywell's disappearance. 'The truth is, I cannot say what happened—and nor can any of us. I think we should wait and hear what the Reverend Hartwell has to say this evening…'

'A capital notion,' Harry said. 'I shall look forward to it eagerly.'

'Are you sure you are well enough to join us this evening?' Beatrice asked with an air of false concern. 'That cough was painful to hear, my lord—perhaps you should go to bed and I will ask Bellows to come and rub goose grease on your chest.'

'No, that you will not,' Harry said, and coughed again, twice. 'I shall drink a little of the excellent brandy Bellows ordered for…us…if I may, and hope that I may be well enough to come down to dinner.'

Beatrice fixed him with a look that would have slain lesser men.

'Pray go on with what you were doing when I arrived,' she said. 'I have no time to waste if we are to have a decent dinner this evening.'

Harry's smile made her turn hastily away. What did he mean by giving her such a look? He was here to persuade Olivia to marry him—not to make her spinster sister's heart behave in the most peculiar way imaginable.

Chapter Six

Beatrice glanced at herself in the mirror as she dressed for dinner. Her one evening gown was sadly worn and out of style. She had refurbished it with a fresh sash and trimmed the edge with green ribbons, but the colour did nothing for her complexion.

Olivia looked at her and frowned. 'I have more gowns than I need, Beatrice,' she said. 'I should have thought before…perhaps some of them could be altered to fit you?'

'I very much doubt it,' Beatrice said and laughed. 'You are a sylph, dearest, while I am what they call well-formed. Do not feel at all uncomfortable because you have a few pretty gowns. They may have to last you for a long time.'

'Yes, I know.' Olivia smiled at her. 'I do not mind that—but I wish I might share those I have with you.'

'It would be too difficult to alter them,' Beatrice said. 'Besides, I shall buy some material soon and make myself a new gown in time for Christmas.'

'Oh, well,' Olivia sighed. 'I do not suppose either

of us will often have much need of stylish gowns in future.'

'Are you feeling very unhappy, dearest?' Beatrice looked at her in concern. 'I know you must miss your friends—but there are some young women in the villages you might come to know in time. Lady Sophia, Annabel Lett, who is a widow and has an adorable little daughter—and Miss Robina Perceval. She is the niece of the vicar of Abbot Quincey and a very charitable and friendly young woman. She sometimes visits our village, and we stop to talk when we pass in the street. I shall invite her to take tea with us the next time we meet.'

'I am sure I shall find friends soon enough,' Olivia said, her blue eyes a little wistful. 'You must not worry about me, Beatrice.' She smiled and tucked her arm through her sister's. 'We ought to go down. Our guests will soon be arriving...'

'I cannot imagine why Mr Hartwell thought it a good idea to visit the Marquis in the first place,' said his wife at table that evening. 'Everyone knows what a dreadful man he is...'

The Reverend gave her a faintly reproachful look. 'I felt it incumbent upon me to make the effort, my dear. Sywell should make his peace with God before it is too late. As a Christian minister, I must do my duty as I see it.'

'Very right and proper,' Harry said, not a flicker in his eyes to betray him. 'Tell me, my dear sir, do you expect the Marquis's demise imminently?'

Beatrice gave him a darkling look. She glanced across the table at her friend Mademoiselle de Champlain. 'Tell me, Ghislaine, how do things go on at dear Mrs Guarding's school? Have you any new pupils?'

Ghislaine was an attractive woman in her late twenties, pleasant to look at but not pretty except for her dark eyes, which were very fine.

'They come and go, as you know, Beatrice,' she said. 'We have several young ladies coming to us after Christmas, and shall be in need of a new teacher to look after the little ones. Have you thought any more about returning to us?'

'I have not given it much thought of late,' Beatrice replied. She saw Lord Ravensden's eyes on her. 'As you know, I have considered taking up a position…if Papa could spare me?' She looked at her father, who was addressing his beef with the dedication of a man who had not eaten such a treat for a long time.

'What's that, Beatrice?' Mr Roade blinked at her. 'Excellent beef, my dear. You and Nan have excelled yourselves…visit Mademoiselle Champlain when you like, have her here to stay for Christmas. Why not? Always pleased to see your friends.' He beamed round the table happily, apparently lost in his own thoughts.

Beatrice would have turned the subject once again, but Olivia was before her.

'Is it true that the Marquis told you his wife had gone, sir?'

The Reverend Hartwell let his solemn gaze rest on

her. A man of forty-odd years, with thinning hair and brown eyes, he was very aware of his importance in the community. The world was full of sinners, and he knew his duty. Let it never be said that he had neglected the spiritual welfare of his parishioners, even one as disreputable as the Marquis of Sywell.

'I do not have to ask where that came from, Miss Olivia. It is unfortunate that Mary Ekins should have overheard me telling Mrs Hartwell…but the gossip will not be long delayed I fear. It is true that Lady Sywell does appear to have left her husband. No one has seen her for months…'

'Why would she do that, sir?' Olivia's blue eyes were wide and guileless, her manner that of a young girl begging for instruction. Mr Hartwell warmed to her at once. 'Do you think the Marquis was unkind to her?'

'How could it be otherwise?' asked the Reverend, frowning and shaking his head sadly. 'The marriage was doomed to fail from the start. Sywell is a disgrace to his class, Miss Olivia—I might say a disgrace to mankind. Far be it from me to condemn a fellow creature, but he was most damnably rude…told me I was an interfering, prosy busybody and…well, such language is not fit for a young lady's ears.'

'No, indeed it is not, Mr Hartwell,' said his wife and smiled kindly at Olivia. 'I dare say you are very shocked by all this, my dear. Pray tell me, have you come home to be married?'

'No…' Olivia blushed fiery red. 'That is…'

'Miss Olivia is not sure she will take me,' Harry

said. 'I have come to beg on bended knee, but she has never yet given me an answer.'

'But I thought it was announced in *The Times*?' Mrs Hartwell stared at him in surprise.

'That was a misprint,' Harry said without the slightest hesitation. 'Dashed awkward for Olivia, you know. I am thinking of suing them…'

'Indeed, you must not on my account, sir.' Olivia gave a strangled laugh, which she smothered behind her kerchief. Her eyes twinkled at him. 'It was simply a mistake, and since I have no wish to marry at all, it cannot make so very much difference in the end.'

'No wish to marry?' Mr Hartwell looked shocked. 'It is surely your duty to marry, my child? It is a woman's allotted purpose in this world, the reason for which all women were created.'

'Oh, but surely…' Beatrice began to protest, then stopped and blushed, remembering the Vicar was her guest, and the rules of politeness would not allow her to disagree with him.

'You wished to object, Miss Roade?' Harry asked, deceptively enquiring. 'I dare say you think a woman fit for other purposes than the rearing of a family?'

'I think a woman should be free to choose whether or not she cares to be married,' Beatrice said, frowning at him severely. 'But I have no wish to argue with our guest, whose opinions must naturally be respected.'

'Just so…' Mr Roade beamed at them all. 'Do we have one of your excellent puddings this evening, Beatrice?'

'Yes, Papa. I shall ring for Lily now…'

She got up and went over to the sideboard, giving Lord Ravensden a look as she passed. He raised his brows at her but she merely shook her head. He was the most provoking man, but she would not be drawn. Time enough for what she had to say to Lord Ravensden when their guests had gone!

'Well,' Olivia said when they were alone in the parlour later that evening, all their guests having drunk tea and left. Mr Roade and Nan had both retired, leaving the three free to speak their minds. 'I think the case plain…Lady Sywell has not been seen in an age. You may depend upon it, her husband kept her a prisoner, and now he has killed her…and this is his way of pretending to the world that she has gone off.'

'You are placing your reliance on the scream Beatrice heard when she was crossing the Abbey lands,' Harry said, nodding thoughtfully. He seemed not to be aware that he had used her first name and Beatrice did not want to be the one to point it out. 'But consider this—the Marchioness has not been seen in months, while Beatrice heard the scream only a few weeks ago. It may be that Lady Sywell found her position intolerable and ran away soon after her wedding.'

'Someone would have seen her,' Olivia said. 'Besides, I have a feeling…' She shivered impressively and looked grave. The great actress Sarah Siddons could not have done better herself had she taken centre stage. 'I am convinced that the Marquis of Sywell killed his wife and has buried her body somewhere...'

Beatrice frowned, remembering the night she had almost been knocked down by the Marquis, who had seemed half-demented. What Olivia was saying was possible. The man was clearly a brute, who cared for no one and nothing.

'Even if you are right...I do not see how it can be proved.'

'We must find her grave,' Olivia replied, a look of determination in her eyes. 'If he has killed her, she must be buried in the grounds of the Abbey.'

'Or the ruined chapel...' supplied Harry, and received a reproving look from both sisters. 'Forgive me, I am sure you are right, Miss Olivia.'

'We cannot look for the grave,' Beatrice objected. 'The Abbey grounds are private property.'

'That did not stop you crossing them...' Harry's eyes danced with wicked amusement, then he crossed his arms and looked penitent. 'But I shall be silent on that subject. What do you suggest, Miss Roade? Shall we call out the militia and demand Sywell be arrested this instant?'

'I told you he takes nothing seriously,' Olivia said to her sister, pulling a face of exasperation. 'How could I be expected to marry a man like that?'

'You could not, of course,' Beatrice said and glared at Harry. 'If you have nothing of sense to say, sir, you may take yourself off to bed. I dare say you are weary, and needing your rest. Shall I send Bellows up to you with a hot posset?'

'A large brandy would be more appropriate,' Harry said. 'But I shall leave you to work out our plan of campaign. You are more in command of the terrain, and I rely on you for instructions. I suppose we shall have to search at night? If we were seen in daylight it might be awkward…or is that a mere quibble?'

'Go to bed, sir,' Beatrice said sternly. 'I shall speak to you in the morning.'

'Yes, Miss Roade. Your wish is my command…' Harry smiled at both sisters and went from the room.

Beatrice looked at Olivia and laughed. 'You are quite right, dearest,' she said. 'He is impossible. I am sure no woman of sense would ever wish to marry him.'

'Perhaps not,' Olivia said, looking thoughtful. 'But for the right woman I suppose he might be an agreeable husband. He is charming, is he not?'

Beatrice turned away to make sure that the fire screen was in place. 'Yes,' she said, without looking round. 'He does have a certain charm, and in some circumstances I suppose a woman might be wise to accept an offer from Lord Ravensden.' She faced her sister, smile in place. 'Come, let us to our beds, Olivia. We must both sleep on all this, and in the morning we can decide what we ought to do…'

Harry smiled to himself as he undressed. His stay in Northamptonshire was proving most diverting. His sense of the ridiculous had made him go along with Olivia's outrageous suggestion, though his own more logical mind told him that it was unlikely they would find a grave…unless, he supposed, the lights in the woods might have a more sinister significance than he had first thought.

It was possible, he imagined, that there might actually be a woman's body buried somewhere on the estate. It was an unpleasant thought, and not one he wished to sleep on.

His mind turned towards the woman he had left downstairs. What was it about her that he was beginning to find fascinating? Far too fascinating for his peace of mind!

Sipping the brandy Bellows had brought him, Harry considered. Supposing Olivia continued to refuse him? He sighed. It was an awkward situation, and he could have wished that things were different. Somehow, he must find a solution to all their problems…

Why was it so impossible to sleep? Beatrice turned from side to side on her pillow, which was unaccountably lumpy. Olivia was sleeping, but as her sister moved she moaned and half woke.

This would never do! She must not wake Olivia. Slipping carefully from beneath the covers, Beatrice pulled on her wrapping-gown and left the room. She normally slept easily at night, but nothing was normal now. Lord Ravensden's arrival had turned their household upside down, and she sometimes wondered if anything would ever be the same again.

Now there was this mystery of the young Marchioness to plague her. Where had she gone? Had she truly been murdered by her cruel husband—or had she simply run away?

Alone in the kitchen, Beatrice poured herself a glass of wine, then saw the glacé fruits that had not been eaten after dinner and helped herself to two of them. They were quite delicious. She ate them both and licked the sweetness from her fingers, feeling guilty as she remembered that she had grumbled at Lord Ravensden for buying them...the provoking man.

How had he managed to get under her skin in this manner? He was constantly making her want to prick at him with words as sharp as needles, and yet she was always glad to see him.

A thought occurred to her, which was ruthlessly denied. Impossible! She could not be developing a *tendre* for him? No, certainly not...such an idea was out of the question. Especially after the way Olivia had spoken of him just before she went to bed. It was clear that her sister was beginning to reconsider...

Beatrice turned her head as the kitchen door opened. Her heart jerked as she saw Lord Ravensden standing there in his silk dressing-gown, his feet bare. He was probably naked beneath that very fashionable robe, just as he had been when she bathed him during the fever.

Beatrice felt her cheeks go warm. She should be ashamed of such thoughts!

'So you could not sleep either,' Harry said. 'May I join you?'

'Yes, of course.' The tray of brandy and glasses

stood on the table with the remains of the nuts and sweetmeats from dinner. 'Brandy is a help when one cannot sleep…and this is a very fine vintage.'

'I am glad you approve,' Harry said. God! Had she any idea of how very desirable she looked in that wrapping-gown? The colour became her so well. She ought always to wear those jewel colours. 'May I?' He poured himself a little brandy into a glass, warming it between his hands as he continued to look at her. 'Do you suppose Olivia is serious about searching for Lady Sywell's grave?'

'Yes, I think she is,' Beatrice said, wrinkling her brow. She was aware of some feeling flowing between them. It had been there for a while now, but she had tried to ignore it. That was easier to do in company than when they were alone, both wearing much less than they ought to be! 'I am not certain that her supposition is correct…but I suppose it could do no harm to look.'

'And if by some remote chance we were to find this grave?'

'Then we should have to call in the militia, Lord Ravensden. It would be a very terrible crime, and the perpetrator should be punished—do you not agree?'

'Your eyes are like emeralds in this light,' Harry said. 'I have never seen a woman with eyes the colour of yours, Beatrice.'

There, he had said it again! Her first name.

'You should not, my lord.' Her cheeks took fire. 'It is not fitting that you should say such a thing to me…'

'It is not fitting that we should be sitting here to-gether,' Harry said, his smile taking her breath. 'But I hope you do not mean to ask me to go away?' Beatrice shook her head. She ought to leave at once herself, but she did not wish to. 'I think we have gone beyond the bounds of conventional conversation, Beatrice. You are a beautiful woman, why do you pretend to be a dowd?'

'I am three-and-twenty, sir. I have no dowry, and I have driven away all the widowers who would have taken me for my usefulness as a mother to their moth-erless children. What use have I for pretty gowns?'

'It is a crime that you should wear grey and brown when you look best in green…or perhaps midnight blue…' Harry considered. 'But you could wear most deep colours.'

'Please be serious for a moment, sir.'

'I am very serious,' Harry said, and pulled a face. 'Must you call me sir? I am Ravensden—or Harry to those I love and trust.'

'To Merry and Lord Dawlish?' Beatrice asked, her eyes raised to his. She caught her breath at the burn-ing heat she saw there.

'And to a few others,' Harry said. 'Perhaps to you one day, Beatrice.'

'When you marry Olivia?' Her eyes challenged him. 'You do mean to ask her again, don't you?'

'I believe I must,' Harry replied and cursed softly. 'We are caught in a pretty coil, Beatrice, are we not? I think I am not wrong in suggesting that you too feel something…'

This conversation should not be taking place! It would not do. She had no idea whether what he had in mind was to offer her *carte blanche* or...but it could not be. He was promised to Olivia, and she believed that her sister would eventually claim her right to be his bride.

'I must go...'

As Beatrice rose so did Harry. He reached out, catching her wrist, making her pause to look back at him.

'I must leave now...'

She got no further, for she was in his arms, pressed close against him so that she could feel the heat of his body. He looked down at her for a moment, then lowered his head, touching his mouth to hers. For a moment his kiss was soft, hesitant, but then, feeling the response of hers, his kiss deepened, becoming passionate, fierce and demanding.

Then, when she thought she would swoon for pleasure, his mouth released hers, and she was free of his embrace. His face was twisted with pain and a hunger that shocked her. Did he want her so very much? No man had ever looked at her in quite that way before.

'Forgive me,' he said, his breath ragged with desire. 'I had no right to do that, no right at all.'

'No,' Beatrice said quietly. 'Nor I to let you. We both know that your duty lies with Olivia, my lord. You are fond of her, and she would make you a fitting wife. Your position demands that, and I have never mixed in society. I am a plain, simple countrywoman, with none of the social arts...'

'As if that mattered…you cannot think it, Beatrice?'

'I do not know what to think,' she said. 'Please, my lord, let me go now. I must return to my sister. To stay longer might prove dangerous for both of us.'

'Harry…' he said hoarsely. 'I beg you, let me hear my name on your lips this once…please.'

Beatrice swallowed hard. 'Harry…' she said, her heart twisting with sudden pain. 'Now, let me go, my dear. You know this is wrong, don't you?'

'Yes.' He stood back, his features harsh, unreadable. 'Had you been any other than Olivia's sister, I might still have found a way…but that is clearly impossible.'

Beatrice turned swiftly lest he should see the pain his words had given her. So he *had* thought to make her his mistress and not his wife. As well then that she loved Olivia too dearly to try and take her fiancé from her!

Harry let her go, and she left quickly, before she betrayed herself. She ran upstairs, feeling the pain too bitter to dwell on. She had brought this on herself, by allowing him too much freedom. He knew that she had done things no respectable young woman would dream of doing, and it had led him to think of her as a wanton.

Raising her head proudly, Beatrice fought down her desire to weep. There was nowhere she could be alone, and besides, she would not weep for such a cause. Had she not been taught a harsh lesson when she was a naïve girl?

It seemed that men were all the same. They used those who were foolish enough to allow them the freedom of their hearts and bodies, and married innocent girls—especially if those girls were heiresses.

She must watch herself in the future. She had let down her guard this evening, but she must keep it firmly in place from now on.

Beatrice watched Olivia and Lord Ravensden laughing together as their relationship developed. The transformation in her sister these past two days was nothing short of amazing. Olivia's imagination had been captured by the disappearance of the Marchioness, and since Lord Ravensden seemed determined to indulge her, she appeared to have lost her shyness with him. She had begun to speak to him in a manner that, if not flirtatious, was certainly that of an intimate friend.

Of course they must have been friends during the Season. Beatrice was beginning to know her sister better, and she sensed that Olivia must have liked Harry Ravensden a great deal or she would not even have considered accepting his proposal. Obviously she had been hurt and deeply distressed by the spiteful tales related to her. However, now that she knew Harry was innocent of the cruel things he was supposed to have said concerning his reasons for marrying her, and that he truly felt some regard for her, she had clearly forgiven him.

Beatrice spent some of her time with them, but she did not always join in their banter. She was trying to keep her distance, and often excused herself on the grounds that she was busy. On Friday and Saturday she attacked the linen cupboards and the pantry with such determination that both Nan and Lily were startled, while poor Ida locked herself in the scullery and would not come out until Beatrice begged her.

However, on Sunday morning she was persuaded to go to church with her sister and Lord Ravensden, and, somehow, on the way home, she found herself walking with Harry. Olivia had lingered to speak with Lady Sophia, who had detached herself from her father, the white-haired, very dignified, distinguished Earl of Yardley, and had come up to them after the service and introduced herself to Olivia.

Beatrice had been delighted that the young woman had shown so much kindness to her sister, and deliberately walked on ahead so that Olivia could spend a few minutes alone with her. She glanced at Lord Ravensden as he joined her

'You have been very busy of late,' Harry remarked, a thoughtful expression in his eyes. 'I must tell you that Olivia and I have worked out our plan of campaign in your absence.'

'Do you really mean to go through with this?' Beatrice raised her eyes to his, then looked away quickly as she saw his expression. He seemed to be reproaching her.

'Why not?' Harry asked. 'What harm can it do? Olivia is determined. I dare say she would go alone if we refused to go with her. Should there, by the merest chance, be any truth in this notion of hers, that might prove dangerous for her.'

Beatrice felt a chill at the nape of her neck. 'Yes, you are very right, my lord. It does seem improbable that the Marquis actually killed his wife, and buried her body…but people are beginning to talk and wonder. I took some shortbread down to Ekins' farm yesterday, and it is true that no one has seen the Marchioness for months.'

'So…' Harry's brow creased in thought. 'It is possible that she has been murdered. And I really do not care for that idea, do you?'

'No,' Beatrice admitted. 'I must say that I should feel both disgust and anger if I thought that she had died at her husband's hands.'

Harry nodded, his expression unusually grim. 'Yes, I imagine you would not wish the guilty man to escape punishment.'

'No, I should not.' Beatrice was thoughtful. 'What have you and Olivia decided?'

'We thought we should take it in turns to walk about the grounds in daylight. Sometimes Olivia and I, sometimes you and your sister, and…' He looked rueful. 'Do you think you could bear to accompany me? I know you must be angry with me for my thoughtless behaviour the other night.'

'Angry…' Oh, if only he knew how much she longed for him to kiss her like that again! No, she must not think of such things. He was forbidden to her by all the laws of decency and truth. She could not look at him as she replied stiffly, 'I am not angry, my lord.'

'Beatrice, you know that I…' Harry broke off with a muffled oath. 'Good grief! I do not believe it. That is Percy's curricle. I would know it anywhere. What on earth is he doing here?'

Beatrice glanced towards her house and saw the smart carriage with huge yellow wheels parked in the driveway. She paused as a man turned and began to wave excitedly at them. Goodness! What on earth was he wearing? His coat was unexceptional, being a very fine blue cloth and cut exquisitely so that it moulded to his slightly stout figure—but his waistcoat was striped in yellow and black, and his neckcloth was so extravagantly high that he must surely have difficulty in turning his head!

'Damn my eyes!' Lord Dawlish exclaimed, striding towards them, a smile that seemed as much relief as pleasure in his dark eyes. 'So there you are, Harry, safe and well. I knew it must be so, but Merry would have it you were ill…'

Harry clapped a hand to his forehead. 'I was engaged to her for Lady Melchit's ball. She will never forgive me. It clean went out of my head.'

'She would have it you were nearly on your death-bed,' Percy said indignantly. 'Made me drive all the way down here.'

'As it happens, she was right,' Harry said, smiling affectionately at him. Percy would not have taken much persuading if he believed his friend was in trouble. 'If it were not for Miss Roade, I might very well have died.'

'You don't say so! You mean Merry was right?' Percy gaped at him. 'Well, I never. I made sure it was all nonsense—but now you come to mention it, you don't look all that clever. Merry would give me no peace until I came to look for you. Your man said you were out of town but refused to say where, and you must know there has been some gossip. That fellow Quindon has been in town, and looking mighty pleased with himself. I dare say he would be glad to step into your shoes. People wondered when you went off without a word, talk of suicide and such nonsense. Never believed a word of it meself…it was Merry who came up with the notion that you might be here.'

'How sensible of you to dismiss such gossip, and how clever your beautiful lady is,' Harry said and grinned wickedly. 'But you have not met Miss Roade…Beatrice, this is my very dear friend Percy Dawlish. I may have mentioned him before, and his wife Merry? Percy, I want you to meet the lady who saved my life.'

'It was no such thing,' Beatrice said with a frown at him. 'My aunt nursed Lord Ravensden, of course. I merely sent for the doctor.'

'Ah yes, of course. I forgot for the moment. It was Mrs Willow who nursed me.' Harry's eyes gleamed. 'It would have been most improper for you to have done so, Beatrice.'

'Yes, I should say…' Percy looked uncertainly from one to the other. Miss Roade did not look quite like the young women Harry usually set up as his flirts, but there was definitely something between them. One only had to look at their eyes, and the sparks were most definitely flying. 'Pleased to meet you, Miss Roade. I must thank you—or Mrs Willow—Merry would be devastated if anything had happened to this rogue here. Very fond of him, though as Merry says, he can be the most tiresome creature.'

Beatrice laughed. She liked this man, who was clearly very fond of Lord Ravensden. For some reason the shadow that had hung over her these past few days seemed to have melted away.

'I am always pleased to meet a good friend of Lord Ravensden,' she said. 'And one who clearly knows him so well.'

'Now, Beatrice,' Harry said, the promise of retribution in his eyes. He was about to say more but his words were lost as Olivia came up to them. 'Percy, you know Olivia, of course.'

'Of course, delighted to see you looking so well, Miss Roade Burton.'

'Miss Olivia, if you please, sir,' Olivia said. 'I do not care to use the name of my adopted family now.'

'Just so…' Percy looked uncomfortable. 'Deuced awkward affair. Can't think what Burton was about to do such a thing.'

'Not awkward at all,' Harry said before she could reply. 'It is all a misunderstanding, Percy. We shall come about, given time.'

Olivia seemed as if she wanted to speak, but changed her mind as Beatrice shook her head at her.

'You will dine with us, Lord Dawlish?' Beatrice said, going forward to smile at him. 'We dine at five and thirty on Sunday. Early I know, but we keep country hours here.'

'I should be delighted to dine with you,' Percy said. 'I noticed a decent inn on the Northampton road. Do you imagine they would put me up for a few nights?'

'A few nights, Percy?' Harry's deep blue eyes quizzed him mercilessly. 'Really? Can you bear it? Northampton, my dear fellow! Will Merry not worry about you?'

'I shall send word that all is right and tight,' Percy replied airily. 'But I think I shall break my journey for a day or two—just to satisfy myself that you are really recovered.'

'Can you be in doubt when I have good friends to watch over me?' Harry grinned at him. 'You always did have a nose for a mystery, Percy. Your curiosity will lead you astray one day, my friend—but if you are to stay, you may make yourself useful. Four of us will discover the grave more quickly—if it is to be found, of course.'

'Grave…' Percy's mouth dropped open. 'No, I say, Harry. Steady on, old fellow. What have you been up to now? Help you all I can, risk life and limb if you needed me—but don't like any of this havey cavey stuff, you know.'

'We are trying to discover if there have been some unpleasant goings on at the Abbey,' Harry said, as they all followed Beatrice into the house. 'Nothing unlawful, Percy…well, only a bit of trespassing.'

'We think Lady Sywell may have been murdered,' Olivia said. 'Pray do tell him, Harry!'

'Yes, I shall do so…' Harry smiled at her. 'It's like this, Percy…a young woman has disappeared in mysterious circumstances. There is a possibility that she may have been murdered…'

'And her body buried in the grounds of the Abbey,' Olivia supplied impatiently. 'All we are going to do is look for signs of her grave.'

'Disappeared…' Percy looked bewildered. 'Don't quite follow you.'

'Do have a glass of sherry and warm yourself by the fire,' Beatrice said, ushering them all into the parlour. 'The Marquis of Sywell is an unpleasant man, you see, and he married a girl out of his class a year ago…and no one has seen her for months.'

'Lady Sophia was telling me that the Marchioness of Sywell did not go into company at all,' Olivia put in. 'Lady Sophia too had heard that the Marchioness has been missing for several months.'

'Sywell…' Percy frowned. 'Know that name… damned unpleasant fellow. Caught him cheating at cards once, never sat down with the fellow again.'

'Did you challenge him?' Harry asked, frowning.

'Not worth the bother, old chap. Only lost a few guineas. Unpleasant thing, calling a fellow a cheat…no proof, of course, just a sense of what was happening.' Percy shook his head. 'Just the sort of chap would murder his poor little wife! Something should be done about it. Damn it all, can't be allowed to get away with that sort of thing. It ain't sporting, what?'

'We are going to try to discover the truth,' Olivia said, smiling at him. 'Would you help us, sir?' She tipped her head to one side, looking so charming that Percy coloured. 'Obviously neither Beatrice nor I can search alone—but if you would accompany me, Harry can protect my sister.'

Percy was irrevocably devoted to Lady Dawlish, but not above a little flattery from a pretty young woman. 'Delighted, m'dear. Of course I wouldn't dream of letting you go alone…if that wretched fellow is about you will need someone to take care of you, see you come to no harm. Delighted to be of service.'

'Thank you, I knew you would not desert me,' Olivia said, and received a wicked smile from Harry as payment for her subterfuge.

Beatrice was a little shaken by this revelation of her sister's society manners. Olivia was clearly nowhere near as vulnerable or as innocent as she had imagined. Her startled eyes flew to Harry, who very reprehensibly winked at her.

'And I shall make it my business to see that Beatrice comes to no harm,' he said, clearly well satisfied with the situation. 'So…when do we commence the search?

'In the morning,' Beatrice said. 'It would not do on a Sunday. Besides, I must see to the dinner. I shall have wine and biscuits sent in to take the edge off your hunger…'

She saw Lord Dawlish send a startled glance at Harry—she could not think of him as anything else since he had forced her to use his name!—and went away, smiling to herself. No doubt Harry's friend would think this a very unusual household…

Chapter Seven

Beatrice sat at the window of the room she shared with Olivia and gazed out into the darkness. Her sister was sleeping, but she had found it impossible to rest, and she dare not venture down to the kitchen in her dressing-robe again, not while they had guests staying.

Outside, the moonlight was turning all to silver, bathing the lawns, trees and hedges in its gentle glow. Beatrice could not help thinking of the evening just past, how pleasant it had been to have company in the house—the kind of company that she found so amusing. Both Lord Dawlish and Harry were great wits in their own way, though she had begun to sense that Harry went much deeper than anyone supposed. However, he was careful not to show his thoughts too plainly, and everyone had spent much of the evening jesting at each other's expense. Indeed, they had been a merry party.

Once, she had looked up to see Harry watching her, and the look in his eyes had made her heart stop and then race madly on. She smiled at her own thoughts, which were far from what a modest young woman's ought to be.

Her smile faded a little as her thoughts turned to the search they intended to make of the Abbey grounds. She knew that Olivia was convinced the young Marchioness had been cruelly murdered, but the idea seemed appalling to Beatrice.

How lonely the young Lady Sywell must have been, trapped in that great brooding house alone with her monstrous husband. Beatrice had never truly thought about it before, but now she felt guilt strike her to the heart. How unkind they had all been! Perhaps if some of the villagers had tried to make friends with her, instead of condemning the marriage…they might have brought comfort to that poor woman.

Sighing, Beatrice forced the unhappy thoughts from her mind and went back to bed. She must get some rest or she would be too tired to do anything in the morning.

'Somewhat neglected, ain't it?' remarked Lord Dawlish as the four conspirators gathered at the Western gate of Steepwood Abbey the following morning. 'Odd sort of place. Almost a wasteland by the look of things, a little sinister, what?' He patted the small but deadly pistol he carried in his capacious coat pocket as if to reassure himself.

'Beatrice and I will walk towards the lake,' Harry said. 'At least we have a good morning for it, no sign of mist or rain. I doubt the grave, should there be one, will be near the Abbey. Too obvious in open ground. No, I believe we should concentrate our search elsewhere.'

Percy glanced round doubtfully. Well enough to speak of searching in the comfort of a warm parlour over a good brandy, but where to begin in what looked to him very like a wilderness?

'Not sure this was such a good idea, Harry.'

'Courage, mon brave!' Harry said and smiled. 'It is a daunting prospect, but reflect, we are simply out for a walk to take the air. Apparently there is only one servant left in the Marquis of Sywell's employ. It is unlikely that we shall be troubled by anyone— and you know what to say if you should be challenged.'

'You and Olivia should try looking in the old herb garden,' Beatrice said. 'It is sadly overrun but still rather lovely, and peaceful. The walls have crumbled in places—but it is not so unpleasant as some of the outhouses, or as dangerous. Many of the older buildings are in danger of falling down.'

'Herb garden, you say? That sounds more the thing, Miss Olivia.' Percy looked more cheerful. It was a bright morning, the sun making the idea of such a walk quite pleasant, and they were all well wrapped up against the wind. He offered his arm to Olivia. 'At least it should be easy enough to spot if the ground has been disturbed. The whole estate has gone wild...disgraceful neglect!'

'Shall we?' Harry offered his arm as they began to

stroll in the opposite direction to their companions. 'Percy is right, you know. This plan was conceived in a spirit of adventure, but it will not be as easy to carry out as Olivia imagined.'

'My sister has not lived here since she was a child, and can have no idea what the grounds were really like,' Beatrice said. She had not taken his arm, she dare not, lest she betray herself. 'My mother's brother adopted her, as you may know. She was too young to understand why she was being taken from her mother, and she sobbed when they carried her away. It was heart-wrenching, so cruel. I have never forgotten the look of reproach in her eyes.'

'But you understood.' Harry's brows arched. 'It must have been a sad wrench for you, to lose your sister.'

'And for my parents. Mama wept for days. I have never really understood why she agreed. Unless…I believe Lord Burton may have paid some of poor Papa's debts. Oh, dear, that sounds terrible! But I think Mama truly believed it was for Olivia's own good.'

'As perhaps it was,' Harry suggested. 'Olivia has had many advantages you have not.'

'Yes, perhaps so, in some ways. We did not see her again for a long time, and when Lady Burton brought her to see us she seemed quite happy. It was only when she was about fourteen that she began to write to me, though I had written to her from the moment they took her from us. I believe, for several years, she was happy enough in her own way.'

'I am sure she was,' Harry said. 'Olivia has been spoiled and petted. I believe Lady Burton at least is genuinely concerned about what has happened. Indeed, I suspect it may have broken her heart.'

'Yes, I suppose it must be an unhappy time for her. It is a pity her husband could not have shown more compassion.'

'I dare say he felt Olivia had let him down. Burton is a proud man—and he had given her everything she could possibly want in a material way.'

'Yes, of course. I do see that—but I think if he had truly cared for her, he might have been kinder. Papa would never cast me off, whatever I did.'

'Perhaps Burton's disappointment was all the stronger, because he had lavished so much attention on her?'

Beatrice looked thoughtful as they approached what must once have been a collection of cottages used by those who served at the Abbey during the time of the monks. Some of them had tumbled down, allowing moss and brambles to grow through the debris. Over the centuries they had been rebuilt and repaired many times, until these past eighteen years when they had been allowed to fall into decay.

'Yes, I am sure of it. But you know, I have been truly loved. I do not think that was the case for my sister—for I am convinced that if they had loved her as they ought, they could not have treated her so shabbily now.'

Harry nodded, but made no further comment. His eyes went over the huddle of ruins with contempt.

What kind of a landowner allowed such wanton waste? He himself had vast estates, which took a great deal of management, but he would have been shamed to see such a sight on his land.

Beatrice saw his look and nodded. 'These have not been lived in for years. No one born locally would come to work or live here after the Marquis's reputation was known. He brought in servants from town for some time, but none would stay long. Even if he wanted to repair his buildings, he would not find anyone here who would work for him.'

'They look as if a good storm would blow them down,' Harry said, frowning at the hovels. 'I shall make a closer inspection. Wait here, Beatrice. I would not have you risk yourself.'

'I am not a child, sir. If you imagine I shall hinder you…'

'Acquit me of such thoughts,' Harry urged. 'Come if you must, but take care. The stones are loose and the ground uneven. I would not have you stumble and injure yourself.'

'Go ahead and I shall follow,' Beatrice said, picking her way over rubble and tufts of grass which had grown up between. A rabbit had started up ahead of them. She wondered suddenly if this was where the rabbits that appeared so mysteriously in her larder came from. It would certainly solve the mystery of the lights in the woods. 'Something has occurred to me, my lord,' she said as she caught up to him. 'I believe Bellows may know these grounds much better than any of us.'

'Now why didn't I think of that?' Harry murmured, a gleam of appreciation in his eyes. 'That was an excellent rabbit pie we had last night...' He looked up as a pigeon fluttered out of one of the ruined cottages and flew off. 'And those pigeons in red wine...quite delicious, and in plentiful supply, one would imagine.'

Beatrice frowned. 'I should have guessed long ago where Bellows was snaring his game, but it was useful and I suppose I did not wish to enquire too closely.'

'A resourceful man, our Bellows. I believe I shall take him into my confidence.' Harry raised his brows. 'You think his loyalty beyond doubt?'

'He has not been paid in three years,' Beatrice confessed. 'I tried to pay him something last Christmas, but he declares he will wait until my father makes his fortune. Which, I dare say, may be never.'

'Oh, I don't know,' Harry murmured wickedly. 'Percy was very taken by your father's idea for gravity heating. Dawlish Manor is very large and very cold. Percy won't go near it in winter.'

'Oh, I do hope Papa will not persuade him to let him try his experiments at Dawlish Manor. I believe it might prove quite expensive, and not at all what Lord Dawlish would expect.'

There was no sign of any suspicious mounds in the ruins of the cottages. After a few minutes, they continued their walk towards the barns and outhouses that had made up part of the monks' working community. During the years of the Yardleys' ownership these had been kept in good repair and used for storing produce from the various tenant farms that still belonged to the Abbey, but the barns too had been allowed to rot and there were gaping holes in the roofs. Some had no more than a wall left standing.

There was somehow a sinister air about the place, an oppressive atmosphere that hung over the huddle of ruins, the smell of age and decay—almost of evil. It was as if a curse lay over everything.

Beatrice shook her head at the thought. It was a foolish one, and should be dismissed at once.

After searching for some half an hour or more, Beatrice and Harry could find no sign of anyone having been near for years. They were reasonably satisfied that there was no grave to be found here.

Leaving behind the depressing huddle of rotting buildings, they began to walk towards the lake. Here there was a gentle undulation in the land, as in much of the county, and they climbed towards the rise, then breasted it to gaze down on the lake lying below. Even the years of neglect could not take away the beauty nature had bestowed on the scene spread before their eyes.

The waters of the lake were grey, reflecting the sky above, but there was a patch of silver far out where the sun had broken through and the surface rippled. Trees gathered about the banks, willows, stunted and shaped by the hand of a cruel wind, reed-beds sheltered water-birds, and beneath the water fish swam, lazily content.

'I have never stood here like this before,' Beatrice

said. 'Whenever I venture on to Abbey lands, which is not often, I always use the shortest route from Steep Abbot to Abbot Giles, and I do not stand and stare. It is very beautiful here…do you not think so?'

'This must once have been a fine estate,' Harry remarked. 'How came it into the hands of its present owner?'

Beatrice began the story, telling it as she had to her sister on the night of Olivia's homecoming, and in this manner they continued to walk, enjoying each other's company, thinking more of how pleasant it was to spend time in this way than anything else, yet taking note of all they saw.

And so it was that they spent nearly three hours exploring, without seeing anything that was in the least suspicious, entirely at one with each other and well content. If in the process they came to know each other's thoughts a little better, then that made the exercise all the more worthwhile.

It was as they retraced their steps towards the Abbey that they suddenly saw someone coming towards them. He was tall, thin, dressed in black, and even before they could see his face clearly, Beatrice knew him.

'It is Solomon Burneck,' she said to Harry. 'He will know me…'

Harry nodded. He linked his arm firmly with hers and went forward to meet the Marquis's servant.

'Good morning, sir,' Harry said pleasantly. 'Forgive me, I believe we are trespassing here?'

'You are on the lands of Steepwood Abbey, which

is the estate of my master the Marquis of Sywell,'
Solomon replied, his narrow set eyes flicking to
Beatrice and then back to Harry, who was so obvi-
ously a gentleman. 'May I enquire your business, sir?'

'Ravensden,' Harry said. 'Miss Roade and I were
out walking my dog and the wretched creature gave
us the slip and ran in here. I am afraid we came to
look for her. We should perhaps have called at the
house to ask permission, but we thought to find her
before we could be a trouble to anyone.'

'A dog?' Burneck's expression did not waver. He
knew true breeding when he met it, as well he might,
and this man was clearly of noble birth. 'May I enquire what kind of a dog, sir?'

'A wolfhound,' Harry replied. 'A great, foolish
creature but of the sweetest temper. I do not suppose
you have seen her this morning?'

'*The way of transgressors is hard*,' said Solomon,
his expression unreadable. 'There are many places
where a creature might lose itself in this wilderness.
It is a place of abomination in the eyes of the Lord.
I fear the curse of ages past is upon this land, and
those who usurp the rightful destiny of others.'

'Yes, quite,' Harry murmured, only the flicker of
an eyelid giving Beatrice a clue to his thoughts at
being addressed in this manner. 'Well, we must tres-
pass no more. We can only hope the foolish creature
will find its way home.'

'*A living dog is better than a dead lion.*
Ecclesiastes, chapter nine, verse four,' Solomon announced, suitably grave. 'God shall punish the unjust

and at the final judgement all men shall be equal in the sight of the Lord. *The Lord giveth and the Lord taketh away.*'

'Yes, you are quite right, it is very true,' Harry said and coughed behind his hand. 'But one must hope for the poor creature's sake that nothing too terrible has overtaken her.' He turned to Beatrice, his eyes alight with wicked mirth. 'Come, Miss Roade. I believe we must delay this gentleman no longer.'

Beatrice inclined her head to Solomon Burneck. She dare not utter a word lest she have a fit of giggles. She managed to contain herself until they had left the narrow lane leading from the Abbey grounds, emerging into a wider road that led either to the village or up the slope to Roade House, then she turned on Harry.

'You wicked, wicked wretch! I thought I should die back there. I do not know how I managed to contain myself.'

'Are you unwell, Beatrice? Where is the pain?' Her speaking look made Harry laugh. 'No, I shall not tease you. I thought Mr Burneck a most unusual man…'

'You must know that Solomon Burneck is well respected by the people of the four villages,' Beatrice said, serious now. 'They believe him to be deeply religious.'

'From his habit of quoting the Bible, one supposes?' Harry looked thoughtful. 'It was all rubbish, you know. Perhaps he does it for effect or…I sensed some deep resentment there beneath the surface, did you? There is something about him, something that seems a trifle unusual, even dangerous. Besides, it does rather beg the question of why such a man chooses to work for Sywell, does it not? If he were truly religious he would surely have left Sywell's employ years ago. Perhaps his master has some hold over him…' He frowned. 'What do you suppose he meant by the curse of ages past being upon this place?'

'How can one know? There are many rumours and tales, but I do not know of a curse…though the history of the Abbey has been bloody and violent, and many who have lived here have suffered tragedy in their lives,' Beatrice said, suddenly realising how true that was. She recalled the feeling that had come to her as they explored the ruins of the old barns and hovels and shivered. 'But Mr Burneck is an odd man. No one truly knows him, except…I have recently learned that he has a cousin, but she married years ago and lives in Northampton. He visits her from time to time, and must presumably care for her. I believe she once worked for the Marquis, though many years ago…'

Harry nodded, and looked thoughtful. 'Some form of blackmail perhaps? The cousin was Sywell's mistress and Burneck stays to protect her reputation for fear of her husband's temper? No, it will not wash, Beatrice. I doubt Sywell would even remember the woman was once his mistress, let alone bother to blackmail her or his servant. No, I believe the man may have some deeper, secret, more personal reason for his loyalty. Something that makes him stay no matter what his master does…'

'Yes, perhaps…' Beatrice was struck by this, which she felt a little sinister. Solomon Burneck was indeed a mystery. She had always been inclined to laugh at the tales told of the Marquis and his evil ways, but now she was very certain that there was indeed something very strange about the Abbey and its inhabitants. She shuddered as the coldness trickled down her spine and spread through her body, then turned to Harry, needing to turn the conversation. 'But why are one's people loyal? I have remarked it on more than one occasion. And Bellows has been as faithful to Papa…'

'But for far more reason,' Harry pointed out. 'Your father is a man anyone would respect and indeed love.'

Beatrice smiled and nodded. She hugged his arm in a companionable way, and felt the chill of horror leave her as her mind returned to normal, happy things.

After leaving Solomon Burneck, she had not let go of Harry's arm and was finding it very pleasant to walk in such close contact with him. It gave her a warm glow inside to know that Harry held her father in such high regard.

'Yes, Papa is very lovable,' she said. 'I have been…' At that moment she saw Olivia and Lord Dawlish approaching from the opposite direction and remembered that Harry was—or ought to be—her sister's fiancé. She let go of his arm. 'Here is my sister…'

The four met, greeted each other with excited cries, then hurried inside the house to warm themselves in front of the parlour fire, which was burning merrily.

'Did you find anything?' Olivia asked. 'We explored the herb gardens—and we walked in the cloisters. We found an open door at the rear and no one was about, so ventured inside. It has the most marvellous arched roof, Beatrice, really very beautiful, but it looks as if it has been used to store broken furniture and rubbish these past years. I wanted to try exploring further into the main building, but Lord Dawlish would not let me.'

'Might have been awkward if we had seen anyone,' Percy said. 'Private house, after all. Wouldn't want anyone wandering into my house without a by your leave.'

'And the Marquis is so often drunk,' Beatrice said. 'You were very right, Lord Dawlish. Besides, I doubt he would have hidden his wife's body in the house itself.'

'Good lord, no! Most unpleasant,' Percy said. 'Enough to give one nightmares, too ghoulish by far.'

'We saw nothing suspicious,' Harry said. 'But we could only cover so much ground, though we walked as far as the lake and returned by another route. I think we need help if we are to succeed in this search. There is still the monk's cemetery and the woods…'

'…the infirmary, which has been used for many years as stables,' Beatrice put in, 'and of course the ruins of the church.' She smiled at Harry. 'Though there is not much more than one wall left standing, I am afraid.'

'If I were going to hide a body,' Olivia said, 'I think I would choose the graveyard…'

'One more soul amongst so many?' Harry nodded. 'Yes, you may well be…' He broke off as the door opened and Nan came in seeming flustered and obviously upset.

'So there you are,' she said, looking at Beatrice a little reproachfully. 'It was while you were all out…I did not know what to do. Bellows had not yet lit the fire in here, and I dare not disturb your father…'

'Whatever is wrong, Nan?' Beatrice looked at her in concern. It was seldom that her aunt's feathers were this badly ruffled.

'He was most put out because I asked him to come back later but I really could not ask him in…' Nan's worried gaze turned on Harry. 'A gentleman, my lord. He said he was looking for you, and when I told him you were out he was…well, he was not polite.'

'What did this gentleman look like?' Harry asked, frowning. 'Pray describe him if you will.'

'He was shorter than you, my lord, and stout—and he had reddish hair cut straight about his ears, in the manner of the Puritans of old.'

'The abominable Peregrine!' chorused Harry and Percy together.

'He insisted he should be allowed to wait, and was not best pleased when I told him he could not,' Nan said, looking guilty. 'But I really could not spare the time to see to him. It was most inconvenient.'

'So you sent him about his business,' Lord Dawlish said. 'Well done, ma'am!'

'The gentleman you speak of was my cousin.' Harry smiled at her reassuringly. 'Sir Peregrine Quindon. Though what he is doing here, I cannot imagine.'

'Come to see if you're still alive,' Percy said with a knowing look. He tapped the side of his nose with his forefinger. 'You may depend he heard the gossip in town, wanted to discover if he was about to inherit your estates.'

'That is most unkind in you, Percy,' Harry murmured reproachfully. 'Peregrine is always most concerned for my health. He never fails to ask me if I am feeling quite well, or to point out that I am looking a little under the weather.'

Percy gave a snort of laughter. 'You may mock, Harry, but that cousin of yours cannot wait for you to die so that he may step into your shoes. If I were you, I should get myself an heir—several of them. Nip his ambitions in the bud, before he begins to get ideas above his station.'

'You do not imagine that Peregrine means me harm?' Harry raised his brows. 'My very dear Percy, you are letting your imagination run wild. My cousin is a bore, and not the most pleasant of companions— but he is far too much of a coward, and of a righteous turn of mind, to do anything violent. If he saw me drowning, he might turn away and pretend he had not seen, but he would not murder me.'

'You are very sure, Harry?' Percy looked unconvinced and frowned.

Yes, I am,' Harry replied. He glanced at Nan. 'I must apologise for my cousin's behaviour, ma'am. I know that Peregrine can be tiresome when he chooses.'

'Well, he was rude, Lord Ravensden, but I was more worried that I might have upset a friend of yours.'

'You did exactly as you ought,'. Harry reassured her with one of his most charming smiles. 'Tell me, did my cousin say where he was going when he left here?'

'Took himself off to an inn, sir. He says he shall return later.' Nan looked to Beatrice for guidance. 'Am I supposed to provide dinner for him? Only we shall be needing more supplies...'

'Allow me to make some provision,' Harry said, glancing at Beatrice, his brows arched. 'My family seems to have imposed itself on your good nature, and I really cannot allow this to continue. With your permission, Beatrice, I shall go myself to Northampton in the carriage this afternoon and bring back what we need.'

'I'll come with you,' Percy said. 'Good grief, yes. We must be eating you out of house and home, Miss Roade, and Peregrine likes his food, none better.'

Beatrice could only smile and thank them for their thought, her cheeks a little warm. 'If you will go, you must take some refreshment first,' she said. 'Excuse me, I shall go to the kitchen and see to it at once.'

Beatrice arranged the silver brushes on the chest of drawers in what had been her mother's bedroom, admiring the impressive Ravensden crest on the backs. She glanced around her. A fire had been burning non-stop for several days now, and the room felt warm at last. The bed was made up with fresh linen and well aired. Harry would take no harm here.

She had moved his possessions herself while he and Lord Dawlish were gone to Northampton. This time she had accepted his offer of help with a good grace. She really had no choice. She certainly could not feed so many guests. It had been difficult enough with one extra gentleman, but it would be impossible with three.

She surveyed her efforts with satisfaction. The mellowed gleam of old wood was somehow welcoming. This was undoubtedly the best bedchamber in the house, well furnished with a cheval mirror, a handsome dressing-chest, an elegant day-bed and a writing bureau; it had indeed been the heart of the house while Sarah Roade lived.

Harry would be comfortable here, and she could go back to her own room. It was not that she minded sharing with her sister, just that she had been restless of late, unable to sleep and worried that she might disturb Olivia.

Beatrice sighed as she gathered up her polishing cloths. Her heart and mind were much afflicted by

what had happened these past few days. The time she
had spent with Harry that morning had served only
to make her realise how very much she liked him.

No, liking was not a strong enough word to describe her feelings for Harry Ravensden. This feeling
she had was very much more than friendship or even
affection. She knew that no man had ever stirred her
senses as he did. She had only to look at him for her
heart to leap wildly in her breast, and the touch of his
hand made her breathless, weak with longing. She
longed for him to kiss her as he had that night in the
kitchen, to kiss her and go on kissing her, to take her
to himself, to his bed, to possess her utterly and make
her his own.

Yet it was not only passion he aroused in her—
yes, she did truly like him as well. He made her laugh
inside. She could share her thoughts with him as she
never had with anyone, except sometimes with her
dear papa. A flicker of his eyelids, a quiver of his
mouth—that generous, soft, oh, so, kissable mouth!—
and she would gladly have surrendered all.

How she wanted to feel his mouth on hers. Her
body felt as if it were melting, as if she were already
a part of him and he of her.

No, this would not do! Her thoughts were immodest. She must not allow herself to dwell on that
wretched kiss. Harry was not hers to love and cherish.

How could she bear to see him marry Olivia?
Beatrice knew that she must stand aside, she must let
her sister choose whether or not she would have

him—but if she did, Beatrice's own heart would break.

Her wandering thoughts were recalled as she heard a man's voice in the hall below. It was loud and complaining, and she knew at once that this must be the abominable Peregrine.

'Harry, you wretch!' she murmured to herself as she went down the stairs. How could he so name his only cousin?

'Ah, there you are, my love,' said Nan, looking at her with relief as she reached the hall. 'As you see, Sir Peregrine has returned...'

'How nice to see you, sir,' Beatrice said, smiling at him. Goodness! He did look very annoyed. 'I am so sorry that no one was here to receive you this morning. My aunt was too busy for visitors—but please, come into the parlour and warm yourself. It has turned colder of late and I dare say you feel the chill.'

'And you are, madam?' Sir Peregrine's gaze narrowed sharply.

'I am Miss Roade. You are in my father's house, sir.'

'Is my cousin here? It is Ravensden I have called to see—and very inconvenient it was, chasing all this way.'

'I fear Lord Ravensden has been called away,' Beatrice replied. 'He and Lord Dawlish will be here soon.' She looked at her aunt. 'Nan, will you bring sherry and biscuits, please?'

'Yes, of course.' Nan went off, clearly relieved to be about her business.

'Come, sir. You must be frozen to the bone,' Beatrice said, leading the way into the parlour. 'Please be seated near the fire.'

She took a seat for herself in a worn leather wing chair to one side of the hearth, gesturing for him to take its twin. Sir Peregrine ignored her invitation and stood in front of the fire, facing out into the room so that she was forced to stare at his profile. He looked about him, clearly contemptuous of all he saw: the shabby furniture, which was a hotchpotch of various styles and periods, worn carpet, faded drapes. Beatrice had grown used to them, but his expression reminded her of how poor her home must look to a stranger.

'It was kind of you to come all this way to see Lord Ravensden,' she said, feeling that some attempt at polite conversation must be made.

Peregrine turned his baleful gaze on her. 'My duty. Only duty, Miss Roade. Lady Susanna Ravensden, Harry's mother, came to see me in town. In quite a way. She had heard gossip. Ridiculous, of course. I told her how it would be. I was sure nothing had happened to Ravensden, and now you see I am right. It was a wasted journey, and in such weather!' He sounded disgruntled…disappointed.

Beatrice was silent. She did not feel inclined to tell this man that Harry had been very ill for three days.

'So…' Sir Peregrine glared at her. 'You are the

sister of Miss Roade Burton—and this is her family home.'

'Yes, sir. This is our home.'

'Quite a come-down for her. I dare say she regrets having jilted Ravensden now.'

Beatrice felt the anger rising inside her. How dare he say such a thing about Olivia? It was despicable. She was not sure how she would have held her temper had the parlour door not opened at that moment to admit Harry and Lord Dawlish.

'At last,' Sir Peregrine said, greeting his cousin with a jaundiced stare. 'I had almost given you up, Ravensden.'

'Had you, Peregrine? How unfortunate.' Harry's brows rose. His manner was cool, reserved. Beatrice was surprised. This was not the man she had come to know so intimately, but she suspected that it might well be the Eighth Marquis of Ravensden. 'Had you notified me of your intention, I might have saved you a tiresome journey. There was not the slightest need for you to come down here.'

'I said as much to Lady Ravensden—but she would have it that something had happened to you.' Sir Peregrine looked outraged. 'She very nearly accused me of having had a hand in your murder! As if I would dream of such a thing. I hope I know what is due to you as the head of the family, Ravensden.'

'I am perfectly sure you do, Peregrine—and I am just as sure that Mama meant nothing of the kind. You know she sometimes gets carried away when she is upset,' Harry said, but there was no laughter in his eyes, only a kind of hauteur. 'However, it was very good of you to concern yourself—and now you may rest easy in your bed, Peregrine. As you see, I am perfectly healthy and amongst friends.'

'Speaking of a bed...' Sir Peregrine frowned. 'The only decent inn in the district has nothing to offer me. I trust you can put me up for the night.'

'This is not my house,' Harry said. For a moment something flickered in his eyes. Beatrice sensed that he was very angry. 'But I believe there may be a spare room.'

Beatrice's eyes met Harry's. 'Do you mean *the* spare room?' He nodded and she almost laughed as she saw the sudden quiver at the corner of his mouth. What was he thinking? The wicked creature! To inflict such a punishment on his cousin! 'Reflect for a moment, my lord. What the probable consequences of lodging Sir Peregrine in such a room might be...'

'Why, what's wrong with the room?' asked Lord Dawlish, sensing their mischief. He had followed Harry into the parlour and they had now been joined by Nan and Olivia.

'It is haunted,' Olivia declared before anyone else could speak. 'By a headless spectre who rattles his chains at midnight and scares anyone foolish enough to sleep there half to death.'

'Ghosts!' Sir Peregrine said dismissively, and looked at Olivia with obvious dislike. 'I do not believe they would disturb me.'

'The room has not been used in years,' Beatrice said with slightly more truth than her sister. 'I do not believe it could be aired in time, sir. Besides, the bed has a broken strut. The last person to spend a night there was very uncomfortable.'

'And took a virulent fever,' added Nan, making everyone look at her in surprise. 'Besides, the sheets have just been washed and there are no dry ones.'

This was most unusual for Nan, and showed that she had taken Sir Peregrine in great dislike.

Sir Peregrine looked horrified. 'Then I shall not stay,' he said. 'I have a delicate constitution. No, Ravensden, I shall not be persuaded. You may give me dinner, I hope? Then I shall return to London. Better to drive though the night than sleep in a damp room.'

'Yes, I am sure you are wise, sir,' Beatrice said and her eyes were drawn involuntarily to Harry. He looked as though he might explode, though whether with anger or some other emotion she could not be sure. 'Now—shall we have our sherry?'

She stayed to drink a glass with them, then excused herself, going to the kitchen with Nan to help prepare their meal, which consisted of a roast, a pigeon pie and a baked carp...supplied by Bellows from where she did not dare think. She spent some time making rich sauces and a choice of puddings. Whatever else Sir Peregrine chose to sneer at in this house, he should not find fault with the dinner set before him.

'That was a splendid meal, m'dear. Splendid!' Mr Roade looked at his eldest daughter with affection. 'Once again you and Nan have excelled yourselves. Now, if you ladies would go through to the parlour, I wish to talk to our guests for a few moments.'

'Yes, Papa, of course.'

Beatrice placed the port and brandy on the table in front of him, then followed Nan and Olivia from the room.

'I shall be glad when that dreadful man has gone,' Olivia said a little later, when they were seated in the parlour drinking tea. 'I cannot like him, Beatrice. Did you hear some of his remarks at dinner? He was so offensive. He almost suggested that I had trapped Lord Ravensden into offering for me. I do assure you, I did not!'

'You should not let him upset you,' Beatrice said and frowned. 'He is clearly eaten up with conceit— and jealousy. Plainly, he hopes to drive a wedge between you and…' She broke off as Sir Peregrine came into the parlour.

'I have sent your man to tell my coachman I am ready to leave,' he announced pompously. 'I fear I cannot stay longer, Miss Roade. My compliments to your cook for an enjoyable meal. I have scarcely eaten better in town. I wonder that such talent is to be found in a village like this.'

His words were uttered in such a manner as to imply that he wondered any decent cook would stay in such a place. Beatrice held her breath and counted to ten. If he had not been Harry's cousin, she might have given him the rough side of her tongue.

'We have many talents in the country, sir,' she said, and stood up. 'I shall see you to the door myself.'

'You are very good, Miss Roade.' He stood back and allowed her to go before him. His cloak and hat were in the hall. He waited for her to hand them to him. She did not do so, and he was obliged to retrieve them from the wooden stand himself. He frowned. 'I must tell you I cannot approve this marriage, Miss Roade.'

'I beg your pardon, sir?' Beatrice curled her nails into the palms of her hands. She must not lose her temper. She must not! 'I fear I do not understand you.'

'The match between your sister and Ravensden was ill-judged. She has jilted him, and no doubt pride brought him here in pursuit of her—but he would be well advised to cut the connection. I cannot think well of Miss Roade Burton.'

'Your opinion of my sister is of no interest to me, sir,' she replied, as calmly as she could. 'If you have anything to discuss concerning Lord Ravensden's marriage, you should properly address it to him.'

'Well said, Beatrice!' Harry came out of the dining parlour. The expression in his eyes shocked her. He was furious. He looked as if he would like to strike his cousin, and was barely able to contain himself. 'Do you have something to say to me, Peregrine? If so, please speak now. But I must warn you, I am at the limit of my patience.'

'I—I must go,' Sir Peregrine muttered, his face pale. 'You are your own master, Ravensden, and have no need of advice from me.'

'Exactly. You would do well to remember that,' Harry said. 'Do have a safe journey back to town, cousin. Should you meet Lady Susanna, please tell her that I am in good health—and very shortly she will have the pleasure of meeting my fiancée.'

Sir Peregrine bowed his head and went out without another word.

'Forgive me for my cousin's disgusting manners,' Harry said, moving towards Beatrice. 'I do apologise for his having inflicted himself upon you. You look pale. What did he say to upset you so much?'

'Only that he could not approve of your intention to marry into my family.' She put her hands to her face, which was burning. 'I know we are not your equal…'

'Have I said that?' Harry looked at her, eyebrows raised. 'Have I ever given you any cause to think that either you or any member of your family was beneath me?'

'No.' Beatrice took a sharp breath. '*You* would not, of course, but I know…'

'What do you know?' Harry asked gently. He took her hands in his, gazing down at her in such a way that her heart went wild, beating against her ribs so madly that she could hardly breathe. 'Had I the freedom to speak as I would like, then you would know, Beatrice. Believe me…'

He was interrupted as Mr Roade and Lord Dawlish came out into the hall.

'Lord Dawlish has agreed to pay my debt to the blacksmith, Beatrice,' her father said, looking delighted. 'That means he will deliver the new parts I need for my experiment. Is that not good news, m'dear?'

'Yes, Papa.' Beatrice looked doubtful and Harry's eyes began to gleam with amusement. 'I do hope so…' she added as her father and Lord Dawlish went into the parlour, apparently on excellent terms. 'Oh dear, how unfortunate…'

'You seem anxious?' Harry looked at her. 'Any particular reason?'

'It is only that the last time Papa fitted his stove, there was an explosion. It blew a hole in the kitchen wall and it was an age before we were straight again.'

'Ah yes, I see,' Harry said. 'We must hope that the improvements work, must we not?' He smiled at her, holding on to her left hand and playing with the fingers. 'Are you feeling more like yourself now, Beatrice?'

'Yes, thank you.' She gave a small, rueful laugh. 'I must tell you frankly, Harry—I cannot like your cousin.'

Harry chuckled, his eyes bright with mischief. 'My very dear Beatrice. No one ever likes the abominable Peregrine. I would have thought it very odd in you if you had.'

'Oh, Harry!' Beatrice's laughter was free of shadows this time. 'You always make me feel so much better.'

'Do I, my dear? I am glad of that.' He let her hand go. 'I think perhaps we ought to join the others, or I might forget that I am a gentleman and must live by the code of honour to which I was born.'

'Yes.' Beatrice's heart raced wildly as she saw his expression. 'Yes, we should join the others…'

Chapter Eight

Beatrice was up early the next morning. She knew the rest of the household would not be stirring yet, and so she slipped out of the house to carry out some of her errands, which had been neglected since Lord Ravensden had followed her sister to Abbot Giles.

There were some elderly folk living alone in the village, in cottages barely fit for inhabitation, and she had always done her best to help where she could. As difficult as things were at times for Beatrice and her family, she knew that some others were far worse off and she always shared what she had; at the moment there were so many good things in the house that she had brought biscuits, cakes, sweetmeats, and some cheese for her friends.

The first cottage she called at was that of Miss Amy Rushmere, a lady who had been a companion to many rich employers during her long and interesting life. Beatrice always called on her at least once a month, staying to drink a little elderberry wine and gossip about what was happening at the houses of the local gentry.

Miss Rushmere opened her door with a smile of welcome. 'Oh, how good of you to come, Beatrice,' she said. 'You must have so much to do with all the company you have staying.'

'Lord Ravensden does not often rise much before noon,' Beatrice explained. 'I think he may be in the habit of riding early when at home, but he still has a slight cough, you know.'

'Yes, I heard that Dr Pettifer had been called out to see him three times,' the old lady replied, shaking her head in distress. 'He must have been very poorly.'

'We feared for his life at one period,' Beatrice said, frowning as she remembered how very ill Harry had been. 'But he is a strong man and I am thankful to say very much better now.'

'Yes,' Miss Rushmere smiled at her. 'I saw you walking together yesterday morning. What a very handsome man he is to be sure.'

'Yes, very.' She sat down at the table. Amy Rushmere was one of the oldest villagers living in Abbot Giles, and there were many things she could remember that no one else knew. 'Tell me, what do you think of the news that Lady Sywell has run off?'

'It is very curious, isn't it?' Miss Rushmere wrinkled her brow. 'Of course, one knew how it would be when he married her. The marriage was always a mistake. She was obviously the by-blow of John Hanslope—at least, rumour would have it so...'

'Have you some other thought on the matter?'

'No, no…I dare say the story is true in this case. I saw her a few times, you know…a pretty child.' Miss Rushmere smiled; her faded eyes seeming to be looking somewhere beyond Beatrice, into the past. 'As a child I used often to walk in Giles Wood, including that part of it which belongs to the Abbey. The estate was very different then, well tended and alive with people. There is a grove in the woods, on the Abbey side, that is said to be sacred, you know…'

'No, I did not know that,' Beatrice said, her interest caught. 'At least, I may have heard it, but I had forgotten.'

'Oh, yes, I know it well from my childhood, and I have been there more recently. It is a pleasant spot and always seems peaceful to me, as if it is blessed in some way. There is a stone, moss-covered, with some strange lettering on it.' Miss Rushmere wrinkled her brow as she recalled something. 'I once saw Lady Sywell sitting alone there. It was just after her wedding. She seemed so sad. I remember her hair was an unusual colour—and she had a delicate, vulnerable look. I spoke to her, but she only smiled. She reminded me of someone, but I am not certain who…I do hope she is safe.'

'Yes, I pray she is,' agreed Beatrice.

Miss Rushmere nodded. 'They do say that anyone who desecrates the shrine is for ever cursed…'

Beatrice felt the shiver trickle down her spine.

'But surely Lady Sywell would not…'

'Oh, no, my dear. I was thinking of her husband. He and his friends were often in the woods when he first came here, and the stories of his orgies are too unpleasant to relate. I think that the spirit of the woods…whoever she may be; I believe it is a woman…would choose to visit her anger more upon the Marquis than his innocent lady.'

'Yes, that would have more justice,' Beatrice said. 'But it is Lady Sywell who has disappeared.'

'Yes, indeed, and one wonders what can have happened to her. I remember the family who used to live there long ago…young Rupert as a boy…'

Beatrice nodded, letting the elderly lady ramble on as she would. She had wondered if Miss Rushmere could throw a little more light on things, and the story of the sacred grove was very romantic—Olivia would love it!—but it did not help to solve the mystery of the Marchioness's disappearance.

After leaving Miss Rushmere's cottage, Beatrice visited two more, but she did not stay to gossip for long, merely handing her gifts over at the door. She was in more of a hurry than usual, and did not at first respond when someone called her name, then she turned and saw the young woman walking towards her, holding a small girl by the hand. The child was perhaps two years old, a pretty little thing with reddish hair, her mother's very much darker and pulled back in a severe style that did nothing for her.

'Oh, Beatrice,' Annabel Lett said as she came closer. 'You walk so fast I thought I should not catch up to you. It is ages since I saw you.'

Annabel was a widow and lived in Steep Ride with only her cousin as a companion. Some people with nasty, suspicious minds whispered that she was not truly a widow, perhaps because her closest friend was Charlotte Filgrave, who the gossips would have it was a fallen woman, but Beatrice ignored such gossip. She liked Annabel and was always pleased to see her, though they did not often meet, unless it was on their walks.

'I have been visiting Miss Rushmere and others,' Beatrice said as Annabel came up to her. 'Now I must get back. We have visitors staying and there is so much to do...'

'Yes, of course, there must be,' Annabel replied. 'I came early because I wanted to ask Dr Pettifer's advice about something. When I go back I shall call on Charlotte Filgrave and Athene...'

'You could come up to the house and take a glass of sherry if you wish,' Beatrice said. She knew that Annabel's situation was very like her own in that there was very little money coming in, and often thought she too must be lonely at times. 'I am sure Olivia would love to meet you.'

'I should like that another day, providing I may bring Rebecca with me?' Annabel replied and smiled as Beatrice bobbed down to say hello to the child. 'I am expected by Charlotte this morning, but do tell your sister she is very welcome to call if she is over at Steep Ride.'

'Yes, of course—but you must come to tea with us one day, Annabel. Olivia will be glad to make your acquaintance. I shall send a note with Bellows.'

She left her friend, who had begun to walk in the

opposite direction and went up to the house. As she did so she was hailed by Lord Dawlish, who had just arrived and was being shown into the parlour. She hurried to take off her bonnet and pelisse and followed him, finding that both Olivia and Harry were already there, sherry wine and biscuits having been set ready on the table.

'Ah, Beatrice,' Harry said with some satisfaction. 'We were just wondering where you were.'

'I had some errands in the village,' Beatrice replied. 'Friends I must not neglect because we have company. I had hoped to hear something that might help us with our investigation, but I did not.'

'Well, I have some news,' Harry said. 'I have spoken to Bellows, and he has agreed to help us. Apparently, he has a few trusted friends. They are going to the Abbey grounds this very night and will cover much of the ground that we would find difficult.'

Olivia had been standing at the window. 'It has started to rain,' she said, coming to sit down on the sofa. She looked disappointed. 'We shall not be able to walk today.'

'I learned something this morning,' Beatrice said. 'It appears that there is a sacred grove in the woods, on the Abbey side. There is an old tale that says if anyone desecrates the grove they will be for ever cursed. Miss Amy Rushmere saw Lady Sywell there once.'

'A sacred grove?' Olivia was entranced. 'How I should love to see it! And a curse—how strange!'

'A sacred grove,' Harry nodded. 'And a shrine to the Earth Mother, I dare say. Perhaps there might also be the remains of a Roman temple somewhere on the estate?'

Beatrice looked at him oddly. 'Why, yes, I've heard it said the monks built on the site of an old temple—what made you say that?'

'One of my interests is the study of old manuscripts and ancient writings,' Harry said with a little smile. 'There are many forms of what are basically the same belief in the power of good and evil. And it is a strange but oft proven fact that the priests of what would seem to be entirely different faiths chose to build their shrines in the exact same places.'

'Why would that be?' Beatrice asked, fascinated more by this new insight into Harry's character than by the study of old religions.

'It is my own opinion that the forces for good and evil are both held within the air, earth, fire, water and indeed, the very stones that form hills and mountains—and that these twin forces are harnessed by us for either the benefit or the destruction of mankind. There may be certain places on this earth where these forces are more strongly concentrated, for instance where there are ancient woods and water...'

'Then do you deny God?'

'No, certainly not,' Harry said, 'for what is our God other than the greatest force for good known to mankind?'

'And the Devil?' asked Olivia. 'Is he also a form-less force?'

'You are thinking of the horned beast?' Harry nodded and smiled. 'I dare say this force could manifest itself in whatever form it chose—perhaps its most dangerous would be the shape of a beautiful woman. Think of Jezebel, Delilah and Salome...'

'You rogue, Harry!' Beatrice cried. 'I vow there have been as many evil men in history as women— you have only to remember that it was a man who condemned Our Lord to death, and a woman he chose to show himself to after the Resurrection.'

'I would not deny it,' Harry replied. 'The fact that God sent our Saviour to us in our own form only confirms my belief in the ability of these forces to take what shape they like. Our Lord came to show us the way, and his message was one of goodness and love. How better can any of us serve our fellow creatures than by doing good and treating others less fortunate than ourselves with kindness?'

Olivia was clearly much struck by his words. Could this truly be the man she had declared to have no depth of soul? Beatrice thought that perhaps his depth of soul and sensitivity was such that they needed to be protected from a mocking world, that perhaps Harry mocked the world lest the world mock him.

'I see I have given you food for thought.' Beatrice smiled. 'Well, I have work to do.' She turned as Harry coughed. 'Are you well, my lord? Were you comfortable last night? You have not taken another chill?'

'I was very comfortable, thank you,' Harry said, smiling at her concern. He had thrown off his serious mood and was once again the man of society manners. 'This cough is a little irritating, but I dare say it will clear in time. I am quite well now. I have a very strong constitution, you know. In fact I am hardly ever ill.'

'I have some syrup of rose-hips that may ease your throat,' Beatrice said. 'I shall fetch it at once.'

She went to the door and was met by Lily, who had been about to knock.

'A note has been sent down from Jaffrey House, miss. It is addressed to Miss Olivia.'

'You may take it in to her.'

Beatrice was thoughtful as she hurried away. If Harry was right…then the feeling of horror she had experienced in those tumbledown buildings at the Abbey might have more significance than she knew.

She shook her head, trying to rid herself of a feeling of foreboding. She had experienced it the night she first visited the Abbey, and it had come to her a few times since.

But this was all nonsense! Harry had probably been mocking them again!

Beatrice went to the stillroom and brought back a small blue bottle and a glass. She poured a measure into it, handing it to Harry, who sipped it cautiously then smiled as he found it both soothing and pleasant.

Olivia looked up from the note she had been reading, an expression of pleasure in her eyes.

'Lady Sophia has asked me to take tea with her this afternoon,' she said. 'Is that not thoughtful of her?'

'Yes, very kind,' Beatrice replied. She saw at once

how much the thoughtful gesture had meant to her sister. 'Perhaps Lord Ravensden will send you in his carriage if the rain keeps up?'

'Yes, of course Olivia may have the carriage,' Harry agreed and frowned because she had used his title, not his name. Now what bee had she got in her bonnet? 'Were you not also invited, Beatrice?'

'Lady Sophia is more Olivia's age,' Beatrice said, avoiding his intent gaze. 'In the past Papa has turned down many kind invitations from the Earl and his family. We could not repay their hospitality, you see, and Papa will not accept charity. Except for the logs, of course, which he does not know about, so cannot hurt him. Besides, I have much to do...'

'I have an errand in Northampton,' Lord Dawlish said suddenly. 'Will you bear me company, Harry?'

'What?' Harry seemed lost in thought. 'Yes, yes, of course, Percy.' He glanced at Beatrice. 'I dare say you will be glad of a few hours to yourself?'

'Yes...' She managed a smile. She could not say what was in her heart, so it seemed best not to say anything. 'Please excuse me.'

She left them and went upstairs to help Lily turn out the bedrooms. However, that done, Beatrice changed her gown and went back to the parlour. It seemed very empty. She thought wistfully how very pleasant the last few days had been with so much company in the house.

She would miss Olivia if she married Harry. Oh, she must not think of him that way! It could only increase her pain. And she was definitely in pain. She had allowed herself to love Harry Ravensden, and now she must suffer for it. What a fool she was!

It was time she wrote to Mrs Guarding and inquired if there might be a position at the school for her—perhaps in the spring. She opened her pretty black and red japanned writing-box and took out her pen, then dipped it into the ink. Having finished her letter a few minutes later, she read it through but did not seal it with wax. It might be best if she spoke to Papa before she sent it off.

She went over to the pianoforte, sat down on the stool and began to play a sad, haunting melody that made the tears rush to her eyes. She stopped abruptly as the feeling of hopelessness almost overwhelmed her. What was she going to do?

'Oh, why have you stopped?' a woman's voice asked, and she turned round, startled to see a stranger in the doorway. A very attractive, elegant lady in her autumn years. 'That was delightful, Miss Roade. You are Miss Roade, of course. Mrs Willow said I would find you here, my dear.'

Beatrice rose to her feet, a little disconcerted. She had never seen this lady before, but somehow felt she knew her…there was something about the eyes, and the soft, generous mouth.

'Forgive me…I do not know who…'

'How foolish of me.' The woman's laughter tinkled like wind bells on a summer breeze. 'Mrs Willow would have announced me, but I heard you playing and crept in so as not to disturb you. There was such feeling in your playing, I was caught by it. I am Ravensden's mother, Miss Roade.'

Yes, of course! She could see the likeness now.

'Lady Ravensden?' Beatrice was suddenly thrust into action. She went forward to welcome her guest. 'Oh, please, do come in. Where are my manners? You must be frozen. Thank goodness we have a decent fire to warm you. I dare say you are exhausted after your journey.'

'Please, no formality. By choice I am Lady Susanna to my friends.' Her smile lit up her face. 'What a sweet girl you are! I have descended on you with no warning, and yet you welcome me with open arms.'

'You were worried about Harry—I mean Lord Ravensden,' said Beatrice, tears stinging her eyes once more. How very missish of her. She blinked them away. 'Of course, *you* had to come.'

'Lady Dawlish sent round to my London house the moment she heard from her husband. She said my son had been ill?'

'Yes, indeed. He was very ill, distressingly so,' Beatrice said, all subterfuge gone as she saw the anxiety in Lady Susanna's eyes. 'I was very worried about him for a time. Pray do sit down, my lady. My aunt will no doubt bring us some tea in a moment— you would prefer tea to wine?'

'Yes, thank you, my dear. Please do go on. You were telling me about Harry's illness.'

'He caught a chill,' Beatrice said. 'He was ill during the night he first arrived, but we did not realise until the next morning. We sent for Dr Pettifer at once, and we did all we could to ease him. He was in a fever for three days, but then it broke and he recovered his strength very quickly. He still has a cough, but he is much better now.'

'Harry always was strong,' his mother said. 'He caught scarlet fever as a boy—from one of the grooms. He was forever playing in the stables! He was very ill and so was his sister Elizabeth. She…died, but Harry recovered and was none the worse. Thank God! I feared that I would lose them both.'

'Oh, so that's who Lillibet was,' Beatrice said as a flash of understanding came. 'In his fever he talked of her and said that it should have been him who died. It seemed to trouble him a great deal.'

'Did he say that he ought to have died in her place?' Lady Susanna stared at her. 'You are quite certain, Miss Roade?'

'Yes. Quite certain. Why? Is it important?'

Lady Susanna nodded. 'Perhaps. I have wondered if he might have blamed himself for his sister's death. He was so very fond of her. We all were, of course, but Harry worshipped her. They were inseparable as children, and I do not believe he was ever quite the same afterwards.'

Beatrice saw the sadness in her eyes. 'Yes, of course. You must all have felt it dreadfully…the loss of a child. Little angel, that's what Harry called her.'

'Indeed she was,' Lady Susanna said. 'I dare say

that's why she was taken so young—she was too
good for this world.'

They sat in silence for a moment, then Lady
Susanna smiled. Her smile was so very like Harry's.

'Well, it was a long time ago, Miss Roade. We
must think of the future. Pray tell me what my son
has done to make your sister cry off? I am sure he
must have said something careless. He does have a
wicked sense of humour.'

'Indeed, he does at times,' Beatrice agreed, with a
look that betrayed much more than she knew. 'But it
truly was not all his fault. You must not blame him
too much. He told a friend in confidence that it was
not a love match, but someone overheard and added
malicious lies to the tale. Olivia was very upset.'

'Naturally, as any young lady would be in her
place.' Lady Susanna frowned. 'I dare say we know
who spread these lies. You may not have heard of
Harry's cousin, Sir Peregrine Quindon. He is a most
unpleasant man.'

'He was here yesterday,' Beatrice said. 'He told us
he had come because you were anxious about Lord
Ravensden and begged him to search for Harry.'

'Indeed, I was anxious when I heard all the stories
circulating,' Harry's mother replied. 'But I did not ask
that odious little toad to search for Ravensden. I
would not trust him in such a case. He envies my son
his fortune and title.'

'Yes, that was obvious,' Beatrice agreed. She liked
Harry's mother, she liked her very much. 'I am certain Harry knows it…' She paused, blushing as she

realised she had used Lord Ravensden's name yet again. 'Forgive me for being so familiar. You must think it strange, but we have been living so close…almost as a family. We are all on first-name terms. But I ought to remember Lord Ravensden's title when addressing a member of his family. It is very wrong of me to presume so much. I do beg your pardon.'

'No, no, my dear, not at all. It is pleasant to hear that Harry has such good friends,' his mother said. 'Sometimes he seems to take nothing seriously—like me, I fear.' She looked pensive. 'Yes, he can be very like me at times.'

'There can be nothing to complain of in that, I am sure.'

Lady Susanna shook her head. 'When the head will not let the heart rule, much can be wrong,' she said. 'I must tell you in confidence…'

They were interrupted by the sound of voices outside in the hall, and then the door opened and Harry, Lord Dawlish and Olivia came in together, all laughing and obviously on the best of terms. They all halted and stared in astonishment as they saw Lady Susanna.

'Mama!' Harry looked astounded as he saw her. 'What are you doing here?'

'Lady Susanna,' Percy said, seeming less surprised than his friend. 'Glad to see you. Devilish cold out this afternoon.'

'Lady Susanna…' Olivia blushed and made a slight

curtsey, obviously a little embarrassed by the unex-pected encounter.

Harry crossed the room and kissed his mother's cheek. 'It was good of you to be concerned for me, Mama, but you should not have come all this way in this weather.'

'Won't like the inn I'm staying at,' Percy said with a frown. 'Very noisy in the mornings.'

'But Lady Susanna will stay here,' Beatrice said at once. 'You can take my room, Lord Ravensden. I shall move in with Olivia—and Lady Susanna may have your room. It is the best, so I am certain you will not mind moving once more.'

'It is not I who will suffer the inconvenience,' Harry said, his eyes warm with approval. 'But if you are certain you do not mind?'

'Of course not. We could not think of sending Lady Susanna to the inn. She will be more comfortable here with us.'

'Then I shall say no more,' Harry said. He smiled at her, then turned to his mother. 'I have been shop-ping this afternoon, Mama. I have discovered a very good linen draper by the name of Hammond in Northampton, and I have bought several rolls of ma-terial. I hope they will please you. I shall show them to you later.'

Lady Susanna looked surprised. 'That was very thoughtful of you, Ravensden.'

'I have also brought gifts for everyone here,' Harry said. 'I bought you a fan and a book of poems, Olivia. For Mrs Willow I have a roll of good woollen cloth in a deep blue colour. I do hope she may find it acceptable. For Percy I bought a pair of York tan gloves. For Mr Roade a case of good port and another of Madeira. For Lily and Ida there are warm shawls. For Bellows a new pair of boots, he gave me his size…' He paused and glanced at Beatrice. 'I bought Miss Roade a new gown. Mrs Willow lent me one of your old ones yesterday, Beatrice, and the seamstress altered something she had made up previously to your measurements. She assured me it would fit you perfectly.'

Beatrice blushed fiercely. Oh, the wicked, devious man! He had gone to so much trouble to cover his kindness, knowing that she would have refused such a gift had he tried to give it to her without having bought presents for everyone else. His thoughtfulness touched her, and she could only shake her head at him.

'You must have spent a great deal of money, my lord.'

'It was just something to do on a wet afternoon,' Harry said. 'Your family has received me—and my entire family—with such kindness and generosity. I wanted to give each of you some small token in return.'

'And so I should think,' Percy said, who had obviously been in on the conspiracy all the time. 'Bought a few gifts myself, Miss Roade. Just gloves and perfumes, you know. Not much good at choosing frippery. Usually leave all that to Merry. Very clever at it.' He looked thoughtful. 'Tell you what, dine with you all tonight, then leave for London in the morning. All right and tight now. Don't need me getting in the way, and Lady Dawlish will be missing me.'

'Yes.' Harry grinned at him. 'Another day and we shall have Merry dashing down here to see where you are. You had best go home and set her mind at rest, Percy.'

'Just what I thought,' his friend said and smiled a little secret smile to himself.

'Well, I must speak to Lily and make arrangements for dinner this evening,' Beatrice said. She glanced round the room at all the smiling, happy faces. 'How pleasant it will be this evening. We shall miss you when you leave, Lord Dawlish.'

'Sorry to leave, Miss Roade, but I dare say we shall be seeing each other often enough in future.'

She could not help feeling a little wistful. It had been so very pleasant these past few days, and the house would seem quiet when they had all gone.

Beatrice nodded but said nothing more as she went out. She supposed that Olivia might ask her to stay once she was married to Lord Ravensden. She must remember to call him by his title! No doubt she might meet both Lord and Lady Dawlish one day. But it would not be the same. Nothing would ever be the same after Harry married Olivia. She could not expect it.

Beatrice left Lily to finish the preparations for dinner and went up to the room she was once again sharing with Olivia. Her sister was already changing into a pretty blue gown. An emerald green silk gown was lying on the bed.

'That must have been made by a French modiste,' Olivia remarked. 'It is quite lovely, Beatrice, and it will suit you. Harry has chosen well—but he is known for having exquisite taste. His house in London is magnificent. I visited only once, but everything is so beautiful.'

Beatrice looked at the gown, then reached out to touch it reverently with her fingertips. She had never in her life owned or worn anything as elegant. Olivia watched her as she hesitated, seeming almost afraid to pick it up.

'Put it on,' she urged. 'He bought it for you. He wants you to have it. You cannot refuse when he went to so much trouble. That would be churlish, Beatrice.'

Beatrice nodded. She could not trust herself to speak, but went behind the screen to wash and change. Some minutes later, she emerged wearing the gown. She glanced at Olivia nervously.

'How do I look?'

'Beautiful.' Olivia laughed and pulled her in front of the dressing-mirror. 'Let me do your hair for you, dearest—and you may wear my amber beads.'

'Do you not want to wear them?' Beatrice asked as Olivia fastened the string of small beads on gold wire about her neck. 'They are so delicate and pretty.'

'I shall wear the cross and chain Mama sent me the year before she died,' Olivia said and bent to kiss her sister's cheek. 'You may keep these beads if you wish. They were a gift from a friend. I left my more expensive jewels with the Burtons. It may have been foolish, but I did not wish to bring them.'

'You were very right to do so,' Beatrice said, as Olivia began to dress her hair in a softer style than she usually wore, allowing curls to fall in charming disarray. 'Perhaps one day you will have pretty things again, dearest.'

'The fan Harry bought me is exquisite,' Olivia said, and showed it to her. 'See…it has gold filigree on the mounts.'

'Very stylish,' Beatrice agreed. She sneaked another glance at herself in the mirror. The gown fitted so well it might have been made for her. It had a dipping décolletage which showed the merest glimpse of her breasts, small puffed sleeves, a wide sash and a skirt that draped her figure so lovingly that it was almost indecent. 'Is this gown a little too revealing, Olivia?'

Olivia was searching in her trinket box. She frowned and pulled open all the drawers one by one.

'I cannot find Mama's cross…' She turned to look at Beatrice and laughed, mischief in her eyes. 'You should see the gowns some of the ladies wear in town; *that* is positively demure!'

Beatrice blushed. 'Sometimes I feel such a country mouse. It is years since I went anywhere.'

'You must have been lonely after Mama died.' Olivia frowned. 'I cannot think where I put the necklace she gave me. I was sure it must be here, but I cannot find it.'

Beatrice saw she was really worried. 'When did you last wear it, dearest? Can you not remember?'

'I am not sure…' Olivia thought for a moment. 'Oh yes, I remember touching it when we were in the herb garden… Oh, I do hope I did not drop it there!'

'Perhaps it is caught on the gown you were wearing,' Beatrice said. 'Leave it for the moment, Olivia, and we will both look tomorrow. If we cannot find it we will go to the Abbey and search for it together.'

'Yes. I would hate to lose it,' Olivia said. She fastened a string of seed pearls about her neck. Then looked at her sister, reaching out to pat one last twist of hair in place. 'You look stunning, Beatrice. I can think of no other word that does you justice.'

Beatrice looked shy as she nodded. Was that really her in the mirror? That elegant, rather attractive lady? Surely not!

'Shall we go down?'

'We must use a little of Lord Dawlish's perfume,' Olivia said, dabbing a tiny dot of perfume behind her ears. 'It was kind of him to think of us, was it not?'

'Yes, very kind.' Beatrice felt the butterflies start up again in her stomach as she and Olivia left the room together. She really felt most odd—like someone completely different.

Everyone had gathered in the parlour to await them. Olivia pushed her forward, making her go in and hanging back so that for a moment she stood alone.

'Oh, Beatrice,' Nan said, the first to speak. 'You look lovely, my dear. Doesn't she, Bertram?'

Mr Roade looked at her and nodded. 'Nice gown, m'dear. You look beautiful this evening—but then, I have never thought you anything else.'

'Exquisite...' Lord Dawlish breathed, clearly amazed by the transformation.

'Quite lovely,' said Lady Susanna. 'That colour becomes you, my dear. Harry has chosen well.'

Harry said nothing. He did not need to, his eyes said it all.

Beatrice blushed and looked away from his intent gaze. Be still her foolish heart! She must not let the gift of this wonderful gown give her hope. Nothing had changed. Harry was promised to Olivia. He must keep his word for the sake of honour, and her sister's happiness.

'Dinner is ready,' Lily announced from the doorway. Her mouth dropped open as Beatrice turned. 'Oh, lor! Oh, Miss Beatrice. You be a proper lady now.'

Beatrice smiled, the tension leaving her. 'Thank you, Lily. We shall come to table now.'

She watched as her father offered his arm to Lady Susanna. Lord Dawlish escorted Olivia, and Harry obligingly offered an arm to both Beatrice and Nan.

'Thank you,' she said softly as he set a chair for her. 'I have never worn anything as lovely.'

'The woman makes the gown,' Harry murmured, a wicked glint in his eyes. 'One day I shall prove it to you, Beatrice.'

Whatever could he mean? She could not look at him as he went to take his seat at the opposite side of the table. What was he suggesting? Did he hope that she would consent to be his mistress after he was married?

Wicked, wicked thing that she was! She was almost ready to agree to such an arrangement if it was the only way she could have him.

Beatrice spent the whole of the next morning baking. Lady Susanna's tray of hot chocolate and fresh, sweet rolls had been taken up to her, and she was not expected down before noon. Harry and Olivia had apparently gone out walking, though whether they were planning to visit the Abbey grounds she did not know.

It was as she was about to go upstairs and change her gown after the morning's work was finished that Harry came in alone.

She looked at him in surprise. 'Is Olivia not with you? I thought you were walking together?'

'I believe she had a prior engagement with Lady Sophia,' Harry replied, looking serious. 'May I speak with you, in private if you please, Beatrice?'

His expression made her nervous.

'Yes, of course, my lord. I shall come into the parlour. Is something wrong?'

Harry followed her into the room. 'You remember I said Bellows and his friends were going to search the grounds last night?'

'Yes, of course.' Beatrice felt a shiver down her spine. 'Has something happened?'

'They have found something in the woods, which

may be a grave. Bellows says that the ground has definitely been disturbed recently. He was up there some weeks ago and the mound of fresh earth was not there then.'

'Oh, no!' Beatrice felt her legs buckle and sat down on the sofa with a bump. She was shocked beyond measure, and the sickness rose in her throat. Although she had agreed to the search, she had never truly expected that they would find a grave. She gazed up at Harry, her face white. 'Do you think…is it really the Marchioness?'

'I do not know,' Harry said, looking anxious himself. 'I must admit it is a possibility now, but we cannot be sure until the ground has been dug over.'

'You are planning to…' Beatrice was filled with a sense of dread. 'Would it not be best to send for the militia and let them investigate?'

'I considered that, but if nothing untoward is found it could be awkward. Sywell is after all a man of some consequence, despite his disgraceful behaviour. I have decided that several of us will go to the site this evening. If we find a body I shall then call in a magistrate and the law will take over. If nothing is found, we may simply go on with the search or abandon it as we choose. But we might search for ever in such a place and never find anything.'

'Yes, I suppose…' Beatrice was uneasy, but she felt that events had moved on beyond her control. 'You will take care?'

'Of course.' He smiled at her. 'Nothing very terrible will happen, Beatrice. Bellows and his friends

know the Abbey grounds intimately. They are unde-
terred by rumours of pagan rituals carried out in the
woods centuries ago, and by the threat of being cursed
for disturbing the old gods, who were there before
ever the land belonged to the Abbey.' His eyes were
bright with mischief. 'That is to say nothing of the
spectres of dispossessed monks that are supposed to
haunt the chapel. I fear our Bellows is somewhat of
a rogue, though I believe he has his reasons.'

Beatrice smiled. She knew he was trying to make
her laugh, to make her forget the true horror of what
was going on.

'Bellows has helped to support us for the past three
years,' Beatrice said. 'But now that I know…I cannot
allow it to continue.'

'Indeed, I think it ought to be brought to an end
before he is discovered and hung for a thief,' Harry
said. 'But do not worry about it, Beatrice. I give you
my word, before I leave Abbot Giles these things will
all have been resolved.'

Beatrice lowered her gaze, her heart beating wildly.
She could not bring herself to ask him what he meant,
and so returned to the subject of the grave in the
woods.

'Have you told Olivia that something has been
found?'

'No—and nor must you, for her own sake.' Harry
grinned ruefully. 'You know your sister. If she suspected what was planned, she would give me no
peace until I allowed her to come with us. She is not

above using all her feminine arts to gain her own way—as perhaps you may have observed?'

'Yes.' Beatrice laughed ruefully. 'I must confess, I was surprised at first, but she means no harm by her flirting.'

'Indeed not,' Harry agreed at once. 'Olivia is a lovely, charming girl. Why do you suppose half the men in London proposed to her?'

Beatrice smiled but did not answer. It was clear to her that Harry was very fond of Olivia.

'She must not be allowed to accompany you this night. It might make things more difficult…'

'I was thinking of her safety,' Harry said. 'Besides, it has turned bitterly cold. She will be far better in her bed—and should we discover the worst it will not be pleasant.'

'No, of course not.' Beatrice, gave a little shudder and looked at him. 'I suppose you will not allow me to come either?'

'I cannot forbid you,' Harry said. 'But I would prefer you to stay here, Beatrice. I shall tell you everything. Have no fear that I will hide anything from you—no matter what we find.'

'Then I shall do as you ask of me,' she said, and smiled at him. 'You must be hungry after your walk, my lord. I shall go up and change my gown, then a light nuncheon will be served in the front parlour.'

Chapter Nine

Beatrice found herself watching Harry all that evening. She could not get the idea out of her head that his life might be in danger. It was foolish of her to worry, she knew, and yet the strange feeling that had so disturbed her the night she crossed the Abbey lands alone at dusk had come back to haunt her. What was it about that place? The tales of fearful apparitions and ghostly happenings had always seemed improbable to Beatrice, and yet now she wondered if Steepwood Abbey and all who lived there were indeed cursed.

She was fearful, uneasy about what Harry and Bellows were about to do that night. Would the old gods be angered by yet another intrusion into their sacred places?

Oh, how foolish she was to be haunted by legends and myths. She was very sure that Harry was not, despite what he had said about the forces of good and evil being held to the earth in certain locations.

When everyone retired to their rooms at half-past

ten, she gave him a speaking look that he met with a lift of his brows. She shook her head. There was nothing for her to say or do. He knew her feelings, and he had asked her to stay home, and she must obey him in this. She had given her word that she would not speak of what was to happen to anyone, and no matter how anxious she was, must keep it.

It was, however, impossible to sleep. She lay staring into the darkness long after Harry had slipped out of the house. If only she could have gone with him! She longed to rise and follow him, but good sense told her that her presence would merely be a hindrance to the men as they went about their gruesome business. Harry was not alone. There were four strong men with him. What could befall him? Nothing, of course.

Yet she could not sleep. Something seemed to hang over her, a premonition of danger for Harry. She could not rid herself of the thought that some harm might come to him at the Abbey.

It was no good! She could not lie here next to her sister while her thoughts were with the men in the woods. She would get up and go downstairs.

It was with the intention of waiting in the kitchen that Beatrice rose, but her feet turned towards the room that had always been her own and was now being used by Harry. Perhaps he had already returned and she would find him there.

She hesitated outside the door, knocked softly and then went in, taking her chamberstick with her. The bed was empty. Harry had not yet returned. She took her candle to the mantle and lit two more, then sat down on a seat in the window. A few minutes passed and she was on her feet again, walking restlessly about the room, which seemed to carry the scent of him everywhere.

She touched his brushes, then picked up his dressing-robe, holding it to her face as she breathed in, inhaling the perfumes of sandalwood and leather. Oh, how she loved this man!

She had never expected to feel this way. It was beyond anything she had ever known.

Beatrice took Harry's dressing-robe with her to the bed and sat on the edge, holding it to her breasts reverently. In that moment she knew that she was ready to sacrifice all for love.

If Harry asked her to be his mistress, she would consent. She could not bear that he would leave and never see her again. No matter what his terms she must accept them, with the provision only that her sister would never know and be hurt by the knowledge.

Smiling to herself, Beatrice laid her head on the pillow. She would rest here and wait until Harry returned...

Harry followed Bellows into the kitchen, where the two men divested themselves of their muddy boots with the use of a very ingenious device, invented by Mr Roade, which only scraped the soft leather of Harry's boots a very little.

'I'll have these cleaned up by morning, my lord,'

Bellows said. 'No one will ever know we were up at the woods tonight.'

'The grave of a horse…' Harry shook his head ruefully. 'I must confess to feeling relieved when I realised what had been buried there.'

'It would have been shocking had we found the young woman, sir,' Bellows said. 'Do you wish the search to go on?'

'I think we must continue it for a while,' Harry said. 'If we abandoned it now, I could not rest easy in mind. It may be that we shall find nothing, but at least if we have tried, we have done all we can.'

'We'll concentrate on the graveyard next,' Bellows said, nodding thoughtfully. 'In daylight it should not be difficult to spot if the stones have been moved. It would be easy enough to add another body and no one the wiser.'

'You must take no risks,' Harry said. 'I would not have your death on my conscience. Nor yet any of your friends.'

'Don't you worry about me, sir. There's only the Crow and the Marquis up there, and Lord Sywell is never sober these days.'

'Well, just be on your guard,' Harry warned. 'Sywell would be within his rights to shoot if he saw you…he must be aware that poaching has been going on in a large way on his estate.'

'There's folk needing food in the village,' Bellows said, and frowned. 'I do not excuse what we have done, for I know it to be unlawful, but—if the Marquis did his duty by the estate, there would be work for many as are near to starving. Besides, begging your pardon, my lord—the game is only going to waste.'

'I shall not judge you,' Harry said. 'You have been a good and faithful servant to Mr Roade and his daughter, and for that I respect and applaud you—but it must stop.'

'I dare say there will not be the need for it in future, my lord.' Bellows smiled. 'May I be the first to offer my congratulations?'

'As to that, I have not yet asked the lady in question.' Harry laughed. 'I see I have no secrets from you, my friend. Go to your bed now, and thank your friends for all they do. They shall be well rewarded, I promise.'

'Yes, sir. We all know that. Good night then.'

Harry nodded as the man went out, then helped himself to a glass of brandy, sipping it as he walked up the stairs. He was thoughtful, relieved that the night's work had not proved as gruesome as he had thought it might. Perhaps Olivia had it wrong; perhaps, as he had first believed, the young Lady Sywell had merely run away from her terrible husband. He hoped it would prove so, for the alternative was unthinkable.

The search would go on until the whole of the estate had been thoroughly covered, but he had no inclination to take a further part in it unless he was forced. If another grave was discovered he would need to be there, of course, to lend authority to the investigation. However, he was more interested now in sorting out this business of his engagement to Olivia. Things could not go on as they were…for everyone's sake. He had taken his time for reasons of his own, but he must do something soon.

Opening the door of his bedchamber, he checked as he saw the candles burning and there, asleep on the bed, Beatrice. How lovely she looked, her hair tumbling about her shoulders, face flushed in sleep. For a moment he wondered if he had come to the wrong room, but there was no mistake. She was fully clothed, lying on the covers. Beatrice must have come here to wait for him.

He set his brandy glass down besides the chamberstick she had brought with her, then walked softly to the bed. Why was she here? He could guess. She must have found it impossible to sleep, knowing what was going on, longing to be with them, yet knowing she would only be in their way. She had risen from her bed so as not to disturb her sister and come here…but why here? Why had she not waited for him in the kitchen?

He sat carefully on the edge of the bed, temptation overcoming his sense of right and wrong as he bent to gently kiss her lips. In seconds she was awake, gazing up at him, still caught in sleep, half dreaming.

'Harry, my love,' she whispered. 'You are safe…you have come back to me…thank God.' And then she put her arms up about his neck, and pulled his head down to hers, kissing him with such fervent passion that his desire for her overcame all scruples.

His mouth devoured hers hungrily. His arms were

about her, crushing her against him. He could feel the thrust of her nipples through the fine material of his shirt and knew that she was aroused. She wanted him as he wanted her.

Harry's tongue invaded her mouth, tasting its sweetness, drawing it into his own. He kissed her throat as her head arched back and she moaned with pleasure, then he pushed back her night-robe and found her breasts, his tongue flicking at the nipples, which were peaked and thrusting for his attention. He laid her back against the pillows, his breathing harsh as he buried his face into the softness of her navel, inhaling the warm, sensuous perfume of her skin.

'I want you so badly, Beatrice,' he muttered. 'God, you are so beautiful.'

'I am yours if you want me…'

He was so sorely tempted. Harry had never felt this way about a woman before in his life. He was burning to make her his own, but even as she lay looking up at him, her eyes drowned in passion, he knew he could not do this. She was as innocent as she was beautiful, he sensed that instinctively, and he could not take the gift she was offering him so sweetly. He had taken her by surprise and she had not thought beyond this moment. He could not take advantage of her.

'No,' he said, his voice made harsh by the wrench of self-denial. 'This is wrong, Beatrice. I will not shame you. I will not anticipate your wedding night by grabbing greedily for the sweetness you would offer me. It would not be right…'

Beatrice stared at him in horror. What was he saying? She had misread his feelings. He did not want
her! He spoke of right and wrong, of shame…when
all she had thought of was her desperate longing to
be in his arms. She would have given all for one night
of love, even if she could have no more—but he had
spurned her offer. He was too honourable a man. He
had drawn back, reminding her of the barriers between them, and she felt the sting of humiliation wash
over her.

'Forgive me,' she said in strangled voice. 'I must
have been dreaming. I did not know what I said…'

And then, before Harry could move to stop her, she
rolled away from him, almost threw herself from the
bed and fled from the room, never stopping until she
reached the safety of the room she shared with Olivia.

He would not pursue her here, she knew. She had
forgotten herself in the heat of passion, but Harry had
behaved with all the true decency and honour she
might expect from a man of his lineage. She believed
he would do and say nothing to betray her…but how
was she ever to face him again?

Beatrice leaned against the bedroom door and
closed her eyes, her face burning. She was trembling,
distressed, ashamed. Oh, why had she been so foolish
as to throw herself at him? How could she have behaved in such a wanton fashion? What must he think
of her?

After a moment, she crept back into bed, lying with
her knees curled up to her chest as the memory of his
rejection overcame her.

She was such a fool to think that Harry cared for her. Why should he? She was three-and-twenty, almost an old maid. Olivia was young and fresh and pretty, and she knew how to behave when a gentleman flirted with her. No man would prefer her to her sister! It was her own foolish heart that had led her astray.

Beatrice had lost her head as well as her heart. She had believed that Harry meant to offer her *carte blanche*. At first she had been upset that he could contemplate making her his mistress, but her desperation to be in his arms had made her deny her own principles.

Well, she was well served for her recklessness. She had made a fool of herself, and she must get through the next few days as best she could. To save them both embarrassment, she would try to keep her distance from Lord Ravensden as much as possible over the next few days.

'Oh, here you are,' Olivia said as she came into the kitchen, where Beatrice had hidden herself the next morning. 'I am sure I lost my cross in the Abbey gardens. Will you come with me to look for it? Please, Beatrice. It means so much to me.'

Beatrice glanced towards the window. It was a bright morning with no sign of rain or mist. She decided a walk would do her good, help to take away the headache that had been with her since she woke, besides, she had promised to help her sister look for the trinket.

'Yes, of course I will,' she said, taking off her apron. 'Let me get my cloak, dearest, and we shall go this minute.'

'Have you seen Harry this morning?' Olivia said as they both went into the hall. She waited as Beatrice put on a warm cloak and bonnet. 'Nan said he was up early and went out riding, but he must surely have returned by now. It is almost time for nuncheon.'

'No, I have not seen him,' Beatrice said. She had not ventured near the parlour all morning, and she did not intend to. She would find a task to keep her busy somewhere. But it was not her sister's fault that she was so unhappy. She linked her arm in Olivia's and smiled at her. 'Now, dearest, tell me how you are feeling. Have you settled now? You are not still angry with Lord Ravensden?'

'No, I am not angry,' Olivia replied. 'It was clearly a misunderstanding—and made worse by the abominable Peregrine. I like Harry. He is kind and considerate, and that careless humour is just a game with him.'

'Yes, I know,' Beatrice said. 'I believe he would make…a comfortable husband. You should think very carefully before you refuse his offer, Olivia.'

'Oh, I shall,' her sister said in a rather odd tone. 'I shall consider any offer Lord Ravensden makes me very carefully…'

Beatrice nodded, but did not reply. They had entered the Abbey grounds now, and were walking down the narrow lane they had taken before.

'You walk on one side,' Beatrice said, 'and I shall

take the other. If we both look carefully, we may find it.'

'I believe it may be in the herb garden, for I was touching it when Lord Dawlish and I stood there talking,' Olivia said, but she followed her sister's action, walking with her eyes downcast in case she should catch sight of a flash of gold. 'I should so hate to lose it, Beatrice.'

There was no sign of the heavy golden cross and chain in the lane that either of the sisters could find, but they continued to trace the path Olivia and Lord Dawlish had followed on that earlier occasion, both walking with their heads bent, eyes searching intently for the necklace Olivia had lost.

The herb garden was neglected, its once neat beds overgrown and forlorn, the walls almost completely gone in some places, but it still retained an air of the peace that the long dead monks must have sought here. The beds had been set out neatly between little hedges, separating the medicinal herbs from those used in cooking, but now it was impossible to tell where one began and another ended.

'We stood by the stone bench talking for a moment or two and I touched the cross…' Olivia gave a sudden cry and ran forward. She stooped down and picked something up, turning to wave at Beatrice who was still lagging some way behind her. 'I've found it…'

Olivia gave a little scream as she turned and saw why her sister had not followed her. She was being confronted by a man dressed in what must once have been a well-cut coat, but was now stained and hanging loose about him, the buttons torn from the cloth. His hair was wild about his face, and looked as if it had not been washed or cut in many months, and he was swaying on his feet, cursing in a loud harsh voice.

She had no doubt that this must be the wicked Marquis himself! Olivia was transfixed with terror as she realised that he was very drunk, and threatening her sister. He had some kind of gun in his hand, a heavy thing with a wide barrel that looked dangerous.

'Damned trespassers,' Sywell muttered drunkenly. 'I'll teach you to come poaching on my land... Hang the lot of you. Make an example to the rest...'

'We are not poachers,' Beatrice said. Her face was pale, but she held her head high. 'Be sensible, sir. We are two women out for a walk. We mean no harm...'

'Damned trespassers,' Sywell said, leering at her. He blinked, obviously too drunk to know what was going on. 'Had enough of this...teach you a lesson...'

He aimed his gun at Beatrice, clearly intending to fire. Olivia screamed loudly, and then suddenly both sisters heard a shout and the sound of thudding hooves.

Turning, Beatrice saw a horseman riding straight towards them. It was Harry! His horse jumped between the tumbled walls with ease, trampling on herb beds and whatever lay in its path as horse and rider charged straight at the Marquis. Harry clearly intended to ride Sywell down rather than let him fire at Beatrice.

She cried out in alarm as Sywell seemed to realise what was happening and swung round to face in the horseman's direction. He took aim once again, but as he did so, Olivia gave a great leap forward and threw herself at Sywell's back. The gun's heavy barrel turned skyward and the shots fired harmlessly into the air, but the noise had terrified Harry's horse and it reared up wildly, in an attempt to unseat its rider. Harry held on desperately for a few minutes, but was thrown violently to the ground, almost at the same moment as Sywell pitched forward in a drunken faint.

'Harry!' Beatrice screamed. She rushed to where he was lying, still and unmoving on his back, his eyes closed, colour white as death. She knelt on the ground by his side, running her hands over his face, forgetting all her feelings of shame and embarrassment in her concern for the man she loved. 'Harry, my darling,' she wept, the tears beginning to run down her cheeks. 'Oh, Harry. Please don't die...I love you so. Please don't die...don't leave me. I cannot bear it if you die...'

Olivia came to kneel down at her side. She looked down at Harry's still form. 'He must have been knocked unconscious by the fall,' she said. 'Stay here with him, Beatrice, and I will run and fetch help.'

Beatrice hardly heard her. She bent to press her lips to Harry's, the tears falling onto his face as she continued to beg him not to die. 'Please don't leave me,' she begged. 'Please live, Harry...live, my darling, live for me.'

Olivia glanced towards the Marquis, who lay where

he had fallen, face down in the herbs that had gone wild. He had not moved, and it seemed clear that he was too drunk to do any more harm.

'The Marquis has passed out,' she said, and got to her feet. 'Stay with Harry, Beatrice. I shall not be long…'

Beatrice was vaguely aware of her sister's words, but she did not turn her head as Olivia began to run. All she could think of was the man who lay so still and pale on the ground before her.

'I love you,' she whispered, stroking his cheek. 'I love you, I love you. Do not leave me, my dearest heart, for I think I shall die if you do. Speak to me, only speak to me…'

Harry's eyelids flickered. He made a moaning sound, then opened his eyes and looked up at her.

'What happened?' He sat up, then groaned as he felt the dizziness sweep over him. 'Now what have you done to me, Beatrice? I feel as if a coach and horses has fallen on my head.'

'You were thrown from your horse,' Beatrice said, sitting back on her heels. 'Do you not remember? The Marquis was threatening me with a blunderbuss and you rode straight at him. He was going to fire at you instead of me, but Olivia rushed at him and his shots went wide.' Beatrice drew a sobbing breath. 'She saved your life because of that, Harry. She saved your life…'

'Good grief! Yes, I think she probably did,' Harry said and sat up gingerly. 'What a brave young woman she is. I must thank her properly.' He glanced round and saw the Marquis lying on the ground. 'Where is she? And what is wrong with him? I do trust Olivia did not actually kill the fellow. That would be a trifle awkward, I fear.'

'I imagine he is in a drunken stupor—and Olivia has gone for help,' Beatrice said, biting her lip as she fought the urge to laugh. 'Will you never be serious, Harry? Do you not realise what might have happened here? I thought you were dead.'

'Did you indeed?' Harry smiled at her. 'Fortunately, that was not the case.' He held out his hand to her. 'Will you help me to rise, Beatrice? I am feeling most odd…most odd.'

She gave him her hand and he pulled himself up, but swayed unsteadily for a moment. 'I think I must put my arm about your waist,' Harry said, a gleam she did not miss in his eyes. 'I may be able to walk if you will help me.'

'Olivia will bring Bellows,' Beatrice said, belatedly remembering that she had meant to stay well clear of him. 'Perhaps you should wait, my lord.'

Harry glanced round. His horse was pawing the ground restlessly some feet away.

'Bellows can bring poor Rufus,' Harry said. 'He has never behaved so badly before, and it was truly not his fault. I think you must assist me, Beatrice.'

'Very well, if you lean on me, we can walk home together.'

'Slowly,' Harry said. 'I cannot walk fast, Beatrice. You must be patient and take your time with me.'

'Yes, of course,' she said, looking at him in concern. 'I think you may have cut your head, sir. There is a little blood trickling down your neck.'

'It feels as if I have split it wide open,' Harry said. 'I shall rely on you to nurse me if I am ill again.'

She had the oddest sensation that he was teasing her, deliberately reminding her of what had passed before. She blushed for shame. How could he? Surely he must realise how awkward she felt after what had happened between them the previous night?'

'I shall naturally bathe your head for you, sir.'

'So we are back to *sir* again,' Harry said and sighed. 'I quite thought we had gone beyond that, Beatrice.'

'Pray do not remind me of my foolishness,' she begged, wishing that she could run off as she had the previous evening but knowing that she could not desert him. 'I had been dreaming. I did not know what I was saying. You should take pity and not remind me of something best forgotten.'

'You dreamt of me, I hope?'

Beatrice turned her head towards him, but he had paused and his eyes were closed as if he were in some pain. 'Does your head hurt very much, my lord?'

'I must confess it does,' Harry replied. 'But I truly believe Sywell would have killed you had I not seen you enter the Abbey grounds. I was some distance away and followed—another moment and I might have been too late. Why on earth did you and Olivia come here alone? Were you searching for that wretched grave again?'

'No...' Beatrice blushed. 'It was for a gold cross

and chain, which were a present to my sister from our mother. She lost it here when she was with Lord Dawlish and was so upset that I agreed to come with her to look for it.'

'Did you not think it might be dangerous? Could you not have told me, allowed me to arrange a search? Consider, Beatrice—if we had found that grave, you would probably have been confronted by a murderer, rather than a drunken sot who was too far gone to withstand a push in the back from a woman.'

Beatrice bit her lip, knowing the rebuke was well deserved.

'From that I gather the grave did not contain the Marchioness's body?'

'It was the burial place of a horse.'

She nodded, relieved it had not been what they feared.

'Yes, I dare say the Marquis has buried more than one mount,' Beatrice said soberly. 'He is what is generally known as a bruising rider.' She looked up at him. 'You realise we must end the search after what has happened this morning? We cannot continue it now. Someone might die and that would help no one.'

Harry frowned. 'Yes, I think you are right. I had intended it to go on—but it is too dangerous. If the Marquis is ready to fire on a defenceless woman, then he would not hesitate to kill Bellows or his friends.'

'I was not defenceless, I had my sister.' Beatrice's sense of humour was coming to her rescue. The warmth of Harry's body pressed against her was making her feel things she had vowed she would never allow herself to feel again, but she could not help herself.

'Yes, I had forgot,' Harry murmured and smiled oddly. 'One more debt I owe Olivia.'

'You should not speak of your marriage as a debt,' Beatrice said, overcoming her own feelings in defence of her sister. 'Olivia is a lovely, generous person, and you have confessed several times that you are fond of her.'

'I do not deny it. I do feel a warm affection for your sister, Beatrice.'

Beatrice saw the hot glow in his eyes, and looked quickly away. How could she be mistaken in that look? Harry wanted her. His kisses had told her that last night, even as his words denied her. How was she to take him? This was unfair!

'You must not tease me, sir,' she said. 'I was foolish last night—but it was because of—of things you had said...'

'I know it,' Harry confessed, his expression becoming serious. 'You should feel no shame, Beatrice. This is all my fault, none of the blame can lie with you. I must make an end to this, put everything straight. This has gone on too long, Beatrice. I must speak to Olivia.'

'Yes, I...'

Beatrice stopped speaking abruptly as she saw Lady Susanna, Nan, Bellows, Lily and even Ida following on behind Olivia.

'It seems the whole household has turned out to rescue me,' Harry said and smiled oddly. 'Truly,

Beatrice, I have never known such devotion in my life, despite all the legions of servants I employ.'

'Are you badly hurt, my lord?' enquired Bellows, coming up to them at the double. 'Let me have him, now, Miss Beatrice.'

'Beatrice and Nan will help me,' Harry said, clearly in charge once more. If he had been feeling dizzy earlier, there was no sign of it now. 'You will find my horse wandering back there somewhere—and the Marquis of Sywell in a drunken stupor. You will oblige me by letting Mr Burneck know his master is lying on the damp ground unconscious, and then you can bring poor Rufus home...'

Harry had been about to say more when they all heard the most tremendous bang. Everyone turned round in time to see a little cloud of smoke issuing into the air from the direction of Roade House.

'Papa!' Beatrice cried. 'He must have fitted the new stove...'

'He was in the kitchen when we left,' Nan said, looking frightened. 'I warned him not to build the fire too high, Beatrice, but he said he wanted to test it to the limit.'

'Take Harry's arm,' Beatrice said, and as Nan did so, she let go herself and began to run towards the back of the house. 'Papa... Oh, let Papa be all right...'

Her heart was beating wildly. Oh, why would her father meddle with such dangerous things? She could not bear to lose him too. If anything had happened to her dear Papa...

As she drew near, she saw someone stumble from the gaping hole in the kitchen wall. His face was blackened with soot, and his clothes had been singed by the heat, but he called to her cheerfully as he saw her.

'No need to worry, Beatrice. I am not hurt. It was just as well everyone else had gone out, though. I think I've done more damage this time than I did before.'

'Oh, Papa...' Beatrice said and uncharacteristically burst into tears. She flung her arms about him, and clung to him sobbing her heart out. 'I thought you might be dead or badly injured...and I really could not bear that.'

'There, there,' Mr Roade said, patting her arm awkwardly. He seemed bewildered by her show of emotion. Beatrice was always so calm and sensible. 'No need to take on so, m'dear. It was just a little bang and some smoke, that's all.'

Beatrice shook her head. Now that the tears had started, she simply could not stop. She realised that she had not cried like this even after her mother died. She had held her grief inside then for her father's sake, but now it was pouring out of her, all the grief and hurt she had held inside her for so very long. Suddenly, it had all become too much to bear.

She turned, instinctively looking for Harry, and then he was there, taking her into his arms, bending to sweep her off her feet and carrying her inside the house and into the parlour, where he laid her on the sofa and knelt down on the carpet by her side.

'I am sorry…' Beatrice wept. 'I cannot seem to stop…'

'I am not surprised,' Harry said gently. 'You have been forced to carry too many burdens for too long.' He handed her his handkerchief, which was very large and very white. 'Wipe your eyes, dearest Beatrice. You have no more need to cry. I am here to take care of you now. You will never be so alone again.'

She looked up at him, her eyes drenched in tears. 'But you cannot mean it,' she said. 'You are promised to Olivia. You must marry her. It is the only proper and honourable thing to do.'

'It might be if I would have him,' Olivia's voice said from the doorway, and they both turned their heads to look at her. She was smiling, a hint of mischief in her lovely face. 'How can my sensible sister be so very foolish as to imagine I would marry a man who is not in the least in love with me? I have known for days that Harry was head over heels in love with you, Beatrice—but until this morning when I saw the way you acted when you thought he might be dead, I did not know how you felt about him.'

'Did you not?' said Lady Susanna, coming to stand beside her in the doorway. 'How odd. I knew it the first time I heard dear Beatrice say his name. And of course, I knew that Harry was in love with her when he bought her that gown.' Her laugh had a merry sound. 'It is the first time I have ever known my son to go shopping without being pushed into it. He must be utterly devoted to you, Beatrice.'

'Mama…' Harry warned, a glint in his eyes. 'No,

really, you go too far…what about that emerald necklace I sent you for your birthday?'

'Which I have no doubt you sent your agent to
order from the very best jeweller in town…'

'*Touché*, Mama!' Harry laughed. 'Well, I must admit I do not normally like to visit any commercial
establishment other than my tailor or my club. Unless
it is to buy a horse, of course.'

Beatrice was blushing madly, her cheeks on fire.
'I… Do you really not want to marry Harry, Olivia?
I was sure you were beginning to change your mind.'

'No, honestly, Beatrice, I do not,' Olivia said. 'I
have been hoping he would not ask me again, but my
answer would still have been no had he done so,
which he has not.'

Harry had risen to his feet. 'Would anyone care to
hear my opinion of all this?' he asked. 'Or have you
all made up your minds already?'

'Surely you are not going to deny you are in love
with Beatrice?' his mother cried. 'Really, Harry, I
cannot think what gets into you sometimes. If you
throw away this chance of happiness I shall wash my
hands of you. Please, I beg you. Do not be like your
father. His father and mine arranged our marriage
when we were born. Your father offered for me before I was properly out of the schoolroom, because
he felt it his duty. He did not love me—and I did not
love him. Fortunately, we became friends in time, and
we both found solace in other people.' She paused,
her cheeks a little flushed. 'I was in love once.'

'Were you, Mama?' Harry was sidetracked by this

startling revelation. 'I never knew that...when?' He
frowned, then nodded to himself. 'Was it with
Lillibet's father?'

'Yes...' She smiled at him. 'If I seemed to show
her favour, Harry, it was because of my darling
Robert. We had a brief affair, and then he died. He
left me his child as a farewell gift.'

'No wonder you were so distraught when she died,'
Harry said and the sadness came into his eyes. 'That
was my fault, Mama. If I had not played with the
children of the grooms, it would not have happened.
It should have been me who died that day.'

'No!' Lady Susanna crossed the room to where he
was standing. She looked up at him for a moment,
then reached up to stroke his cheek with her hand. 'I
would have been equally as grief-stricken whichever
of my children had died. I loved you both so much,
though I fear I did not show it enough. I had learned
to discipline myself, you see. It was the only way I
could live. I was tied to a man who was my friend,
but who did not love me—and the man I loved so
very much was dead. How could I dare to show love?
When Lillibet died, I felt that she had been taken from
me in payment for my sins. If I had shown too much
love for you, you too might have been taken from
me...'

'Mama...' Harry stared at her. He was clearly very
moved by this dramatic declaration. 'I never dreamed
you felt this way...'

'How could you?' she asked, and smiled at him.
'You learned by my example, Harry. You learned to

hide your feelings, to protect yourself against love…but I do most humbly beg you not to do so now. If you do not ask Beatrice to marry you, you will lose the most precious thing you are ever likely to possess in your life.'

Harry was silent for a moment. He looked down at Beatrice, and then at all the expectant faces. Behind his mother and Olivia were grouped Nan, Mr Roade and the servants.

'Bellows, you were sent to fetch my horse. Please do so at once,' he said, establishing his authority. 'Mrs Willow, you will oblige me by making some tea for Beatrice, and take Lily and Ida with you if you please…'

'Yes, of course, my lord.' Nan smiled and turned to shoo the gaping servants ahead of her.

'Mr Roade, I would much appreciate it if you could organise both Lady Susanna's coachman and the one I hired in Northampton. I believe we should all remove to my house in Cambridgeshire as soon as possible, for there will not be much comfort to be found here. As cold as my house at Camberwell is, we can reach there before nightfall and be assured of a warm welcome if I send a groom ahead. Bellows may stay here to arrange repairs, and the servants can send our baggage on with the carter tomorrow…'

'Ah yes,' Mr Roade said, his eyes brightening. 'Is that the house you told me was so very old and draughty?'

'I have several old and draughty houses,' Harry replied serenely. 'Do not despair at today's failure, sir. I dare say if we give the matter some thought, we shall discover where your calculations went a little awry…and in time we shall be sure to hit on the answer.'

'Yes, I am almost sure I know already,' Mr Roade said and beamed at him. 'I think we shall get on very well together, Ravensden. I see that you are a man of excellent sense. I knew how it would be the day you came. Did I not tell you that Beatrice would make an excellent wife?'

'Yes, indeed you did, sir.'

Mr Roade nodded as if he had arranged it all, looked kindly at his daughter and went out of the room.

'Miss Olivia,' Harry said and smiled at her. 'It is and has been my intention for some time to make you an offer…not of marriage, but of my friendship. I intend to settle ten thousand pounds on you, money that cannot be taken away from you should I suddenly lose my mind and decide I do not care for the colour of your gown. I do hope you will be kind enough to accept this offer. It sits ill with me that I have been the cause of your downfall and I must—I must!— make some reparation for my own peace of mind.'

'I thank you for your kindness, Lord Ravensden,' Olivia said, and dimpled prettily. 'I shall not refuse your generous offer, for it will make me independent—and you must know that I have made up my mind never to marry…'

'Olivia…' Beatrice said, looking anxious. 'Surely one day…'

'I shall not marry, unless I find a man I can love as much as my sister loves you, Harry,' she said and gave them her sweet smile. 'I shall go upstairs and pack a few necessities for our journey. Lily can help me. We will pack your things as well, Beatrice—and I am sure Nan will be pleased to help Lady Susanna.'

'Thank you, Miss Olivia,' Harry said. 'No, dash it all—why stand on ceremony? We have fallen into the habit of first names, why should we change it now?'

'Why indeed?' Olivia said, 'especially as I expect to hear that we shall be related by marriage very soon.'

'Olivia!' Beatrice protested. 'He has not asked me yet.'

'I have not yet had the chance,' Harry said. He looked at his mother as Olivia went out. 'If you imagine, Mama, that I intend to ask Beatrice to be my wife with you watching, you are very wrong.'

'As long as you do it,' Lady Susanna said. 'I shall take no other for my daughter-in-law, dear Beatrice.' Her laughter tinkled. 'And now I really must go or I do believe my son will lose his temper…'

'Harry…' Beatrice murmured and he looked down at her as his mother left and they were at last alone. 'You must not mind them. They are all so interested in what is going to happen, you see. Even poor Lily and Ida.'

'The house will be repaired as I have said,' Harry told her. 'The servants will have a place here—unless you choose to take them with you, of course. Others will be employed as Bellows sees fit. Mrs Willow will have sufficient money for all that is required to run the house properly. Your father will have a home with us, naturally, but he must also have this house so that he can feel independent and come here when he chooses…besides, I dare say it has many cherished memories for him.'

Beatrice reached for his hand and held it tightly. 'How thoughtful you are,' she said, her throat tight. 'But you do not really mean to let him experiment in your house?'

'My house in Camberwell is ancient and hardly worth preserving,' Harry said and grinned at her wickedly. 'Wait until you have experienced how cold it can get. Only Ravensden itself is bearable in the winter. I prefer my house in town. Believe me, my darling. Your father will do us all a favour if he manages to blow Camberwell up. We shall then be able to build a modern house, which will be very much warmer.'

Beatrice laughed. Her tears had all dried long since. She got to her feet, gazing up at him uncertainly. It seemed that she was to be given all her dreams, and she found it hard to believe even now.

'Do you really want to marry me, Harry?'

'How can you doubt it, my dearest?' He took her hand, carrying it to his lips to kiss the palm. 'I think I have loved you, if not from the moment we met, at least from the moment you came rushing into my bed-chamber with your hair wild about your face. Indeed, I fell in love with you when you tended me as I lay so ill…'

'You called out for Merry,' Beatrice said. 'I wondered if she was your mistress, but then you told me she was Lord Dawlish's wife.'

'There have been women,' Harry said, his gaze narrowing as he looked at her. 'But none I loved. Mama was right. I chose not to let love into my life, because I was afraid of it. I loved Lillibet and she died. I thought that if I let myself love again…'

'Yes, I understand,' Beatrice reached up to touch a finger to his lips. 'I was hurt once when I was very young, and I thought that I would never love anyone again. I did not realise then that he had hurt my pride more than my heart. You taught me what real pain is, Harry. I thought my heart would break when I believed you would marry Olivia—and I was desperate when you were thrown from your horse this morning.'

'I heard you beg me to live.' He smiled tenderly at her. 'I must confess that I was not as badly shaken as I allowed you to believe.'

'Had you not recovered, I believe I should have died…but I knew it was your duty to ask Olivia, and that I had no right to love you.'

'At first I really thought I had no choice but to beg Olivia to be my wife,' Harry said. 'I had given my promise to your sister, and because of my carelessness, Lord Burton threw her out—but then I began to realise that I could not marry her when my heart belonged to you. And yet it was too soon to speak to you. I had to wait in all decency…' He gave her a rueful look. 'Besides, I was not even sure my feelings were returned. It was only when I kissed you and felt your response—then I knew that some other way of settling the affair must be found.'

'Oh, Harry…' Beatrice smiled through more tears. 'I ran away last night because I was so ashamed of what I had done…offering myself to you so shamelessly.'

'And I wanted to take your sweet offer,' Harry murmured throatily. 'I wanted it so badly, Beatrice— but I was ashamed that I could contemplate such a thing. I have always followed my own code of honour in these matters. I knew you to be innocent, and that is the way you shall come to me as a bride. Untouched and lovely as you are.'

'You have not asked me yet,' she reminded him, afraid that she might weep if she did not laugh.

Harry chuckled, and dropped to his knees. 'On behalf of myself, my mother and all other interested parties, I do very earnestly beg you to do me the honour of becoming my wife, Miss Roade. I have a very high regard for you, indeed the highest, and should you refuse, I shall be cast down into the depths of despair.'

'Will you never be serious, Harry?' Beatrice asked, giving him a speaking look. 'I have a good mind to refuse after such a proposal. Indeed, it would serve you right if I kept you dangling for months.'

'But you do not intend to do so, do you, dear heart?' asked Harry as he got to his feet. 'You do know that if you do not this instant consent to be my wife, I shall very likely take you upstairs by force and make love to you until you surrender.'

Beatrice gurgled with laughter. 'You tempt me, sir. If you make such threats, I shall very likely hold out just to see…'

Harry pulled her into his arms and kissed her so thoroughly that she could hardly breathe. She gazed up into his eyes as he released her.

'You are sure you want to marry me?' she whispered, a teasing note in her voice. 'You are not just saying this to please your Mama?'

'Beatrice…' Harry threatened. 'I am counting…'

'Oh, very well,' she cried. 'If it is the only way to save my virtue, I accept.' She laughed as his eyes took fire. 'I accept with all my heart, with my mind and my body…'

Chapter Ten·

'You look beautiful,' Olivia said as she finished arranging the lace and veiling on Beatrice's bonnet. 'And your gown is lovely—as elegant I am sure as Madame Félice would have made it herself if she had not been too busy to oblige you.'

'Lady Susanna was most put out because she could not see me,' Beatrice said and laughed. 'But I did not mind. Madame Coulanges was kindness itself, and I am well satisfied with my trousseau. I have never owned so many beautiful things. Harry is always buying me something…a trinket or a jewel or some little thing that happened to catch his eye.'

'And why not?' Olivia said, sparkling at her. 'You deserve everything he gives you, dearest. For years you had nothing, and now you will have everything money can buy.'

'And more,' Beatrice said, her eyes glowing with the knowledge that she was truly loved. 'You will come and stay with us sometimes, Olivia?'

Beatrice looked anxiously at her sister. Roade

House having been restored, Olivia had chosen to live there with her father at their home in Abbot Giles. She had even declined to accompany Beatrice and Lady Susanna to London when Beatrice went up to buy her bride clothes.

'Of course I shall, often.'

Beatrice smiled as she looked round her old bedroom. She had chosen to be married in Abbot Giles, and her wedding was this very morning. Lady Susanna had wanted to give them a grand reception in town, but Beatrice had begged to be allowed a quiet wedding in her own village.

'I should like my friends to see me wed,' she'd said, a little shyly for her. 'Later perhaps, you could give a ball for us in town, Mama, and all your friends can attend that?'

'An excellent idea,' Harry agreed instantly. Beatrice must of course have her way. 'You could not deny Ida and Lily the privilege of attending you on your wedding day, could you, my love?'

'They will naturally want to see me leave for the church,' Beatrice replied, shaking her head at his levity. 'And to share a piece of the wedding cake, of course.'

'Shall you make it yourself, dear heart?'

Beatrice threw him a darkling glance. 'I shall not have time.'

'Indeed, you will not. The very idea!' cried Lady Susanna, scowling at her son. 'It will take us all our time to be ready, since my impatient son says he will wait no longer than Christmas to claim his bride—though how he expects to have everything ready by then, I do not know.'

'Sooner if I could persuade Beatrice,' Harry said. 'Gowns can wait. Beatrice has the rest of her life to visit the seamstress if she so chooses.'

Beatrice had merely smiled. Her wedding day had seemed an age away then, but the trip to town had been as hectic as it was enjoyable, and before she really knew it they were back in Abbot Giles.

And now it was her wedding day, the twenty-second of December. Beatrice glanced at herself in the mirror once more. Her gown was fashioned of a soft cream velvet and heavily trimmed with a slightly paler lace. Her rather fetching bonnet was trimmed with matching lace and deep blue ribbons.

Harry still preferred her in green, and indeed several of her new gowns had been made in varying shades of green. However, she thought that the soft cream was very suitable for her wedding—its purity reflecting her innocence. For she was still untouched. Harry had managed to restrain himself—though with mounting difficulty.

They were to spend their wedding night and the first few days of their married life at Camberwell, which Beatrice had found a very comfortable, pleasant house despite all Harry had said to its detriment. Harry had employed a small army of craftsmen to make the house as comfortable as possible for them.

'We shall visit each of my estates in the spring,' he had told her. 'But I dare say we shall spend much of our time in town. Unless you particularly wish to live in the country, my love?'

'I can be happy wherever you are, Harry.'

'Perhaps I shall build us a new wing at Ravensden,'

he said, and kissed her hand. 'We have our whole lives to decide.'

They did indeed have a lifetime to decide where they would make their home. Beatrice could hardly wait for the moment when their life together would really begin.

'Are you ready, dearest?'

Olivia's question recalled her wandering thoughts. She glanced at her reflection, touching the simple string of pearls that had been Harry's gift to her on their official engagement, besides the magnificent ring of emerald and diamonds that he thought fitting for his future wife. She knew that there were many precious heirlooms awaiting her in her husband's bank in London, but the pearls had been a personal gift, unworn by any other Ravensden bride.

'I chose them myself,' Harry had told her as he placed them tenderly about her neck. 'I did not send my agent, I promise you.'

Beatrice smiled at the memory. She looked at her sister and nodded. 'Yes, I am ready,' she said. 'Let us go down now.'

In the hall below, family and servants were gathered together to watch her leave.

'Lor, miss, you do look lovely,' said Lily.

'Her be a real ladyship now,' said Ida, sniffing. 'Her won't be with us never no more.'

'You must both stay here and look after Papa,' Beatrice said, smiling at them. 'Do not imagine you will never see me again. I shall return now and then to see all my friends, I promise.'

'You are beautiful,' Nan said, and pressed a posy of silk flowers tied with blue ribbons into her hands.

'I always hoped you would find a good man, my dear, and you have.'

'Yes, I know.' Beatrice smiled and kissed her cheek. 'And he is not in the least addled in the wits.'

She turned to her father. 'Papa, shall we leave?'

He offered his arm. 'Be happy, my dear,' he murmured as they went out to the carriage which was waiting to carry them to the church. It was a very smart affair with the Ravensden coat of arms painted on its side and was one of Harry's many gifts to his bride. 'But I know Ravensden will look after you.'

'You will come and stay with us often, Papa?'

'Most certainly. I have almost perfected my idea for gravity heating, Beatrice. I have promised Ravensden that I shall make Camberwell as cosy as you could desire. I dare say I shall be ready to begin work in a few months…just as soon as you two have had a little time alone together.'

Beatrice smiled. She faced the thought of her father's assault on Camberwell bravely. After all, Harry had promised that they would go on a tour of his estates as soon as the weather improved. That should take several weeks, and there was always the lovely and comfortable house in town.

Harry and Lady Susanna were guests at Jaffrey House. When the Earl of Yardley had heard that Ravensden and Beatrice were to be married in the church at Abbot Giles, nothing else would do for him.

'I knew your father, Ravensden,' he had told Harry. 'You and Lady Susanna will oblige me by staying here for a few days—and I shall be delighted to offer you my house as the venue for your wedding reception.'

Harry had accepted the offer in the spirit in which it was made, bringing in an army of his own servants and cooks to prepare the meal that was to be offered to their guests. Beatrice's quiet wedding had become rather larger than she had anticipated. However, since the guests invited were, apart from Harry's friends, to come largely from the four villages, she could not complain.

'We shall give food and ale to everyone who comes to ask,' Harry had said when telling her of his plans. 'Ours shall be a wedding that every man, woman and child in the four villages may enjoy if they wish.' He smiled and kissed her. 'I want everyone to share in my happiness, Beatrice. When I first came to this place, I expected to be bored—but I have never known a dull moment since I arrived. I am very grateful to the people of the villages for giving me my lovely bride.'

Beatrice had invited several children from the villages to be her bridesmaids, and Olivia would have charge of keeping them in order, something that would take some doing! Beatrice's wedding had set the four communities buzzing, and there was sure to be a great deal of talk about this day for months ahead.

There was a large crowd gathered outside the church to watch Beatrice arrive, despite the fact that it was a chilly morning. A cheer and then the sound of clapping greeted her as she stepped from the carriage. Inside the church there was not one spare seat to be had. Beatrice was more popular than she would ever have guessed, and everyone was delighted that she had made such a fortunate match.

Beatrice was vaguely aware of how many people had gathered to see her wed, but once she entered the church, her eyes were only for the man who stood waiting for her to join him. He turned as the organ music announced her arrival, and the love in his eyes brought her to the verge of tears.

She walked, head high, on her father's arm to join him.

'So…' Sir Peregrine said to Beatrice at the reception later. 'I must wish you happy, madam.' It was clear that the words stuck in his throat. 'At least Ravensden has chosen a sensible woman this time. I suppose I may be certain of a decent dinner should I choose to visit you.'

'Of course, sir,' Beatrice said and smiled. Even his poisonous barbs could not spoil her happiness this day. And all of Harry's other friends had greeted her with true pleasure, especially Merry Dawlish, who was already planning a long visit in the spring. 'Anyone Ravensden or I choose to invite to our home may be sure they will be welcomed in every way possible.'

She did not add that she would be glad to welcome him, and he gave her a sour look before walking off to speak with Lady Susanna.

Harry came up to her a moment later. 'What did the abominable Peregrine have to say?'

'Nothing that need make you frown so, my dearest Harry. You need not fear for me. I was vulnerable when your cousin stayed with us, but I can assure you, I am well able to deal with him now.'

Harry's eyes gleamed. 'You will oblige me if you

can persuade the abominable Peregrine not to visit us more than once every five years.'

'Harry!' she scolded laughingly. 'I hope I know my duty to your cousin better than that—however abominable he may be. He shall come and stay when Merry does, later in the spring.'

'But do you know your duty to me?' Harry asked, his eyes beginning to smoulder.

'I believe it is to love, honour and obey…' Her eyes met and challenged his. 'I shall try to be a dutiful wife, my lord.'

'Then do you think you could manage to say your farewells and slip away quite soon, Beatrice? I should like to be alone with my bride.'

'I shall do as you bid me, my lord.'

'I wonder…' Harry laughed. 'This is a new Beatrice indeed. It will be interesting to see just how long this meekness will last.'

She shook her head at him and went away to change her gown, refusing to be drawn. It would hardly befit the new Lady Ravensden to admit that she was as impatient as her lord.

Nan and Olivia were waiting to help her with her clothes. There were hugs and kisses, and good wishes, then Beatrice came down to where a little group of young women from the villages were waiting to see her leave. They looked at her expectantly as she held her posy of silk flowers out, then laughed and threw them in the direction of the young women, but it was Olivia who caught them neatly.

Harry, meanwhile, had been throwing handfuls of coins to the young urchins who had gathered in anticipation of the custom, and were now scrambling eagerly on the ground in pursuit of the silver and gold.

Beatrice laughed with sheer pleasure at the sight, then she was being helped inside the carriage, a final wave and they were on their way.

'At last,' Harry said as they stood together in the small, comfortable parlour he had requested should be made ready for them. A good fire was burning in the grate, throwing out a welcome warmth after the chill of the journey. A cold meal and wine had been laid on the table, and, except for Harry's valet and Beatrice's maid, the servants had retired for the night. 'Come here, Beatrice. I want to know just how willing you are to serve your lord.'

Beatrice laughed as she heard the teasing note in his voice. She was wearing a very elegant travelling-gown of heavy silk in a deep shade of green, and her hair was dressed into the loose curls her maid had spent so much time arranging earlier.

'Very willing,' she said, and stood laughing up at him. 'What is it you would have of me?'

Harry reached out and began to take the pearl-headed pins from her hair. He dropped each one carelessly on to the floor, letting each strand fall until it was free. Then he ran his fingers through her hair, satisfied only when it became a wild tangle.

'There,' he said huskily. 'That is the vision I saw when I came back from that hell of pain—the sickness that would undoubtedly have claimed me had you not saved my life.'

'I did only what any other woman would have done...'

'No! You did far more—more than I had any right to expect,' Harry said, a look of tenderness in his eyes. 'You gave me so much...even then, when you scarcely knew me. Why? Why did you do that, Beatrice? You had no reason to care whether I lived or died.'

'I would not have had you die in Papa's house— whatever would people have said?' Beatrice asked, but the teasing look disappeared from her eyes as she looked into his. 'Or perhaps I loved you from the start. The first time I saw you—before I knew your name.'

'But you tried to send me away...'

'You had hurt my sister. I denied my heart. I believed you must be the monster who had so carelessly destroyed her.'

'When did you change your mind?' Harry looked at her intently.

'When?' Beatrice began to smile, the wickedness in her eyes. 'Why, my lord—I believe it was when I pulled back the covers and saw you...' She paused and blushed.

'...naked?' Harry laughed, his eyes taking fire.

'As nature intended.' She gazed up at him naughtily.

'I believe I have got me a wanton wench!'

'I believe you may have done,' Beatrice admitted. 'Are you very hungry, my lord? Only I do not particularly wish for supper.'

'I am hungry only for you,' Harry said, and reached for her. His kiss was both tender and passionate, full of an aching yearning. 'I believe I should like to go to bed, Lady Ravensden.' He smiled as he released her. 'Go up now, my love, and I will follow shortly.'

'Yes, my lord,' Beatrice replied, her manner so demure that his eyes gleamed with laughter, knowing full well that some wicked barb was to come. 'But I pray you—do not be long lest I fall asleep.'

There was no fear that she would fall asleep. Beatrice allowed her maid to help her into the gossamer-soft garment she had chosen for her wedding night, before dismissing the girl with a smile. She sat before her dressing-mirror, brushing her own hair as she had always done, then went to the bed and lay down.

When Harry entered the room, she closed her eyes. She did not need to see him to sense that he was near. He sat on the edge of the bed as he had once before, gazing down at her, then she felt the touch of his lips on hers.

Opening her eyes, she smiled up at him. Very slowly, she reached up and slid her arms about his neck, pulling him down to her. This time when they kissed, Harry did not restrain himself. His need was such that she felt the power of it, and when at last they drew apart, both were trembling.

'I love you, Beatrice,' he murmured huskily. 'I love you more than I can express in words. Will you let me show you in the only way I know how?'

Her eyes darkened and grew smoky with desire. 'I love you, my dear, dear Harry. Show me how to be a good wife to you. Teach me what you would have me know and be.'

'I do not believe you will need much teaching, my

wanton wench,' Harry murmured throatily as he reached out for her. 'But I promise you, I shall be a demanding master.'

Then he was pulling her gown over her head, discarding it with his own robe so that she was free to touch the wonderful smooth skin she had once tended so lovingly while he lay in his fever. There was no need of tuition on either side, for they each knew instinctively what would please the other.

'So lovely, so lovely,' he murmured huskily. 'As I always knew you were beneath those hideous gowns. It is the woman who makes the gowns, Beatrice, but this skin is too lovely to be touched by anything but pure silk. You are the goddess of my heart, and everything I have is yours to use as you will,' he vowed, and buried his face in the sensuous satin of her flesh.

Breast to breast, thigh to thigh, they caressed and kissed, playing each other like fine instruments to make sweet music. Harry's lips and tongue sought out the secret, sensitive places of her body, lavishing her with such tender, loving caresses that she was swept away with him to pleasure beyond all imagining. And if there was a moment of pain when at last he entered her, making her truly his own, she was scarcely aware of it. She was a woman made for love and loving, and she opened to him with all the warmth of her being, feeling only the joy of being truly loved, of belonging. They were joined as one: one heart, one body, one mind, one soul, and both knew that to find such completeness was a blessing from the gods that was not given to all, and believed themselves the favoured ones.

And after their first coupling was over, they lay

entwined, talking long into the night as lovers will, confessing all their secrets that neither had ever told so that they were irrevocably bound. He came to her again and again during that night, taking her with tenderness sometimes, at others with a fierce passion that left them both exhausted, so that at long last they slept deep into the morning.

And their servants crept about the house and smiled to know that master and mistress were still sleeping.

My Lady Ravensden was sitting up in her bed amongst a pile of silken pillows. She had been married a month now, and was blissfully content. Her tray of hot chocolate and sweet rolls had been brought up, together with a small pile of letters.

Beatrice saw that most had come from the villages. There was one from Ghislaine, one from Olivia, and another from her dear papa. What a feast awaited her, for she knew that both Ghislaine's and Olivia's letters would be full of lovely gossip, and she was anxious to hear the latest news and whether anything more had been discovered concerning Lady Sywell's disappearance.

She opened Ghislaine's letter first. Her friend wrote such a clear precise hand, and her letters were always so entertaining. If anything had happened at the Abbey, she would be sure to have news of it. And indeed, it seemed that there were at the moment some very interesting happenings.

'Still abed, you lazy wench,' Harry said, coming in as Beatrice was about to reach the meat of Ghislaine's letter. 'It is far too good a morning to lie abed. Get up and come riding with your lord.'

'Yes, Harry, in a moment,' Beatrice said. 'I just want to read what Ghislaine says…'

Harry plucked the letter from her grasp. She tried to take it back, but he withheld it, so she sat back and looked at him, giving in to his mood of playfulness. He would no doubt return it in a moment.

'Ghislaine says there is news of the Abbey…'

Harry was not attending her. He had begun to fold the paper into a shape that looked rather like an arrowhead, sharp at one end and flaring out wider at the other. Lifting his arm, he drew back the paper dart then brought his hand forward and released the paper with a strong thrust. It flew straight across the room and into the open grate, where it was consumed in seconds by the flames.

'Harry!' Beatrice cried. 'I hadn't finished reading my letter.'

Harry's expression was one of astonishment. 'Did you see that, Beatrice? Did you see the way it flew straight and swift?'

'Straight into the fire,' Beatrice said. 'You wretch.'

'How wonderful it would be if man could build a machine that would fly…'

'You mean a balloon?'

'No…' Harry was still wearing that look of amazed wonder. 'Balloons travel at the behest of the wind, and are awkward, clumsy contraptions. I mean a machine with some kind of energy that man can direct and control…' He turned to her, suddenly excited. 'I recently bought a collection of papers from the estate of a man who had travelled widely; he was a scholarly man, well versed in ancient scripts—and among his papers I saw a fragment of parchment with what looked like the beginnings of a design for such a machine. I do not know where the paper came from, or who scribbled the few details upon it, but I believe it might possibly be made to work. I must write to Mr Roade at once and tell him of my idea before I forget.'

'A flying machine, Harry?' Beatrice looked at him in amusement. 'Would that not be rather dangerous?'

'Slightly less so than a stove that overheats and blows holes in the kitchen wall,' Harry said wickedly and bent to kiss her. 'Just think what fun Papa and I will have trying to discover if the contraption will fly.'

Beatrice smiled at his enthusiasm. She had little doubt that this would be the first of many inventions that Harry and dear Papa would waste their time on in the years to come, but as long as they were content, what did it matter?

'Now what is going on in your head?' Harry asked and bent to kiss her. 'I am going to write my letter; will you be long, dearest?'

'I shall join you in half an hour,' Beatrice promised. 'Go down now, my love, and let me finish my letters—what there is left of them.'

'I am very sorry that I threw your letter into the fire,' Harry said, and kissed her hand. 'Will you forgive me?'

'You are already forgiven,' she said and smiled as he kissed her hand once more, then walked over to the door. 'I shall not be long, Harry.'

Beatrice picked up her remaining letters as the door closed behind her husband, but she did not attempt to open them. She was so very lucky…but the letter from Ghislaine had reminded her, and she could not help thinking of the young Lady Sywell. They had not been able to find a grave, and the mystery of the Marchioness's disappearance was not yet solved, but Beatrice could not forget the unhappy young woman.

What had happened to her? Had her wicked husband murdered her—or had she left Steepwood Abbey of her own accord? Beatrice had no way of knowing. She would no doubt hear from one of her friends if there was any news, but she was no longer living in the villages and it must be for others to discover the truth.

Beatrice shook her head, dismissing the shadows as she rang the bell to summon her maid. It was time that she got dressed and went down to go riding with her beloved husband!

*   *   *   *   *

MILLS & BOON®

Makes any time special™

Mills & Boon publish 29 new titles every month. Select from...

Modern Romance™   Tender Romance™

Sensual Romance™

Medical Romance™ Historical Romance™

MAT2

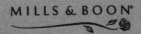

MILLS & BOON®

Historical Romance™

A TRACE OF MEMORY by Elizabeth Bailey

A Regency delight!

The Earl of Wytham is suspicious when a bedraggled woman accosts him in his woods claiming to have lost her memory. His first thought is that this is yet another ingenious matrimonial ploy. But when her beauty and her vulnerability become an increasingly alluring mix, can they resist their longings, because each unfolding memory suggests that she could belong to another man!

LORD FOX'S PLEASURE by Helen Dickson

The Restoration of Charles II
…secrets, intrigue and conquests…

The Restoration of the monarchy meant a time to take stock for wealthy landowner Lucas Fox. The pleasure-seeker wanted a wife and it was the proud, impulsive Prudence Fairworthy who caught his eye. But with her suspicions over his motives and the mystery surrounding his past, Lucas knew she would not be easily tempted by marriage. But there was untold pleasure to be found in the art of persuasion…

On sale 1st June 2001

Available at branches of WH Smith, Tesco, Martins, Borders, Easons, Sainsbury, Woolworth and most good paperback bookshops

0501/04